JUDITH

THE CASE OF THE CAMPUS CAT

Judith Wolf

CRANTHORPE
—MILLNER—
PUBLISHERS

First published by Cranthorpe Millner Publishers (2024)

ISBN 978-1-80378-221-8 (Paperback)

www.cranthorpemillner.com

Cranthorpe Millner Publishers

Printed and bound by CPI Group (UK) Ltd
Croydon, CR0 4YY

MIX
Paper | Supporting
responsible forestry
FSC® C013604
FSC
www.fsc.org

For
Felicity Riddy

PROLOGUE

As far as Morgan Byrd was concerned, the story began when Alka-Seltzer went missing; but in the weeks leading up to his disappearance, four other women found themselves increasingly troubled by recurrent dreams, while one small boy was awake after midnight and busy with a secret mission.

A darkness of creepers and branches hiding the more luminous darkness of the sky. The rapid scuttle of a lizard. The smell of her own fear, acrid on her skin. The elderly woman stirring restlessly on the bed is restored by the grip of her dreaming mind to the youthful vigour of fifty years ago, a vigour which inside the dream is all expressed in a tense and desperate stillness. Her senses are alert to catch a sound, a sight, a scent which may warn her of approaching danger. As she crouches, every muscle taut, she is panting silently. Her heart thuds against her side.

1

There are flashes of light, now, in the darkness. The whiplash crack of gunshots. The crackle and dusky glow of flames. She begins to slither cautiously on her belly, holding her breath as if it were a spell to conjure silence, back towards the huts. Back towards the heart of the nightmare. As she nears the clearing, the screaming begins.

She wakes to the familiarity of pain, lived with so long by now that it is almost reassuring. She accepts it, as she accepts her pounding heart and sweat-drenched skin. The nightmare, too, is something that she has lived with for most of a lifetime. Sometimes months go by without its returning, but the decision she has recently made has brought it back in all its original vividness and terror. She knows that, until she has completed the task she has set herself, it will visit her nightly. This too she accepts.

Easing herself painfully out of bed, she reaches for her stick, pulls on her dressing-gown. Sitting at the kitchen table, her hands clasped for warmth round a mug of tea, she faces the future and renews her determination. Unconsciously, as she summons up her forces to meet what is to come, her face clenches into the implacable grimace of a tribal mask.

The sickly whimper and burning forehead of the child. Back and forth, back and forth in the darkened bedroom, carrying that fragile burden, murmuring to him, trying to soothe him into stillness. The darkness without matching the darkness within, an arid, empty blackness where once a great light shone. The refusal of her struggling mind to relinquish the loved thing that her arms enfold. He cannot ask it of me. He cannot. He cannot ask it of me.

She no longer knows whether she is arguing with God or with the man she is trying not to wake. The man in the double bed, the man by whose side she has slept for all these years. Barren years, and now the fruit of her aging womb, the firstling of her heart, is to be torn away from her. Worse, is to be sacrificed by her own hand. And she cannot do it.

No, it is not even that she cannot. She will not. She refuses. She will not do it. Love and anger conspire within her to cast out faith. She will not consent to the sacrifice. Like Lucifer, she will not serve.

She wakes to hear the echo of her own voice screaming, 'He's not yours, I tell you. I don't even know who his father is. You've got no part in him. He's not your son.'

She is walking down the aisle of an enormous supermarket, searching the shelves with feverish anxiety for something she has forgotten, something nameless and desperately needed which she knows she cannot live without for even a moment longer.

The objects on the shelves shift and dissolve under her gaze. Faceless shoppers block her way as if from deliberate malice. The aisle divides into a labyrinth of pathways. Impatience and rising panic thrust her on.

Neon lighting glares down coldly on the scene like light reflected from snow. As if that chill illumination has summoned it up, she finds herself gazing into an enormous cold cabinet. The thing she has been searching for is lying in the bottom of it, swaddled and white and still.

As always, the nightmare fails to wake her. She turns over in her sleep, letting the oblivion which lies between dreams wipe away the image, absorbing its horror back into her subconscious mind.

In her dream, the girl is lying awake in the same narrow bed in which she fell asleep. Around her, the room is familiar and calm. She sees the desk with its orderly array of notebooks and pens, the books ranged neatly on their shelves, the posters pinned to the wall. There is nothing here to threaten. She is safe in the present tense.

Somehow, though, her bed has become twisted around. She ought to be facing the curtained square of the window. Instead she is staring at the door, a door which begins to open, slowly, slowly. She feels fear run through her veins like freezing water. Her heart seizes up. Her mouth opens into a black oblong, as wide as the black oblong of that gaping doorway. Her own silent scream is choking her, but she dare not let it out.

His whisper is in the room with her, intimate, caressing, obscene. She becomes aware, as his voice engulfs her, that her bed has the high, hinged sides of a cot.

As he does now every night, the boy wakes and feels in the darkness for the borrowed and hidden old iPod and headphones. Careful not to make a noise, he climbs out of bed, thin and bony in his striped pyjamas, and pads barefoot over to the window-seat. Sitting up very proud and straight, soundlessly mouthing the syllables, familiar by now in their strangeness, he wills himself to listen and remember.

Outside, on the moon-streaked rooftops, a cat yowls its barbaric song. Alka-Seltzer, blissfully unaware that his rapidly approaching fate is to be the stuff of national headlines, is acting out his normal springtime urges of passion and conquest.

CHAPTER ONE

Morgan Byrd ranked sleep pretty high on the list of the major sensual pleasures of life, and unlike the rest of the list you didn't even need to be conscious to enjoy it. On this particular morning she was dragged reluctantly up from its downy depths by the sound of Lin's voice, toneless and loud and horribly insistent, repeating her name. Her spoken name, which Lin hardly ever used except at moments like this. Signing, for all its undoubted eloquence, cannot penetrate slumber.

Morgan peeled her eyelids apart and looked at the old-fashioned alarm clock which stood on a tin tray on the bedside chest. Lin was standing next to it, holding out a plate and a mug in hands already streaked with paint. She had probably been working since half past six. She looked amazingly beautiful. Morgan looked at her with exasperation mixed with desire.

'For God's sake, Lin,' she said crossly, 'it's the bleeding dawn. It's Saturday. It's the vacation. It's ...' Memory returned, and with it a rush of panic. 'Oh Christ, it's that conference! Why the hell didn't you wake me?' Even as she said it, she dimly recalled punching the alarm clock into silence at some half-conscious moment in the recent past.

Lin's face said, 'Why do I put up with you?' She dumped the plate and mug on the chest. Her hands said, 'Drink your coffee, Bird. And get a move on, you're late.' Her face said, 'I love you.' She left the room.

Morgan took a gulp of coffee. It was extra strong and extra sweet, Lin's way of kick-starting her into the day. Morgan said, 'Jewish mother, yet,' and wandered through into the bathroom, still clutching the mug. She inspected her bleary reflection in the mirror, sluiced her face with cold water, brushed her teeth, took another gulp of coffee. A nasty combination of flavours, but at least she was now awake.

Back in the bedroom she dressed fast – blue jeans, silk shirt, velvet jacket, earrings, high-heeled boots. She ran her fingers through her short hair, took the stairs two at a time, grabbed the folder with her conference paper from the kitchen dresser, glanced at her watch. She would just make it.

Starting the car, she wondered for the thousandth time why she had let Lin persuade her into living in this God-forsaken spot. Yearning for city streets and their unnatural grime, she drove through the budding and burgeoning green of the spring landscape towards the coast and the university campus.

She arrived at the Arts Building with less than ten minutes in hand. She had meant to use them to take a quick glance through her paper, but instead she was waylaid by Collington, the university porter.

'Morning, Dr Byrd, miss. I was wanting a word.'

Morgan sighed and glanced at her watch. 'Can't it wait, whatever it is? I'm due at a conference session.'

'Gender and role-play in thingummy wotsit, is that, miss? I'm just on my way to unlock the room. The other young ladies mostly isn't here yet. But I was hoping to catch you, see. It's that Alka-Seltzer. He's gone missing again. So if you could maybe keep an eye out for him.'

Alka-Seltzer was the campus cat. He was a large, un-neutered ginger tom whose tattered ears attested to the riotous nights and worse for wear mornings-after from which he had got his name.

'He'll come home when he feels like it, surely. He always has before.'

'Well yes, miss,' said Collington doubtfully. 'Only it's that young Oliver, see. He will have it as he's been kidnapped, miss.'

'Ollie Cresswell?' Morgan was unable to keep the irritation out of her voice. 'Don't tell me Daphne has taken to arranging classes for him in the vac, now.'

'No, miss. Not that I know of.' Collington's voice was complacent with the certainty that very little went on around the university without his being aware of it. 'He's been coming in mornings to feed Alka-Seltzer, being as Dr Blair-Guthrie's in South America.'

Nobody owned Alka-Seltzer, but years ago he had chosen to take up residence with the venerable Dr Elspeth Blair-Guthrie in her campus flat. And since the idea of Alka-Seltzer in a cattery was unthinkable, someone always had to be found to feed him whenever Elspeth was away. Morgan thanked her lucky stars that this time it wasn't her.

She said, 'He can't have been catnapped. Who on earth could possibly want him? Ollie's just looking for attention. But I'll keep an eye out anyway. Look, shouldn't you be unlocking the lecture-theatre? It's nearly half past.'

'I'll see to it right away, miss.'

Morgan drove home at the end of the afternoon in an unreasonably bad mood. The first day of the early feminist fiction conference had been a complete success and her own rather provocative paper on the polarisation of female roles in Robert Bage's *Hermsprong* had produced both a flatteringly heated debate and an offer of publication in a quite prestigious women's studies journal; yet she was feeling as scratchy and irritable as Alka-Seltzer after a hard night on the tiles.

The thought of Alka-Seltzer seemed to crystallise her discontent. Over sixty years of feminist struggle, she told herself crossly (or over two hundred and sixty years, depending on when you started counting), and you still had an entire university campus making a mascot out of a wretched tomcat simply because it embodied all the worst excesses of stereotypically male behaviour. Not to mention the absence of most of her own male colleagues from any conference which involved women's issues. Like the one she had just been attending.

Morgan swung the car into the narrow road which ran through Hangman's Wood. The sight of the trees with their dense undergrowth of flowering weeds reminded her of Lin. Lin, with her quietness, her stillness, her calm certainty about who she was and what she wanted, her honesty. Morgan realised that she had been deceiving herself about the causes of her ill temper. It was not so much the absence of her male colleagues as the presence of one of them. Or rather, of one of them and his baby.

Rupert Allison was the latest of Morgan's male colleagues to discover the belated joys of parenthood. To Morgan's jaundiced eye, the entire campus seemed to be full of first-time fathers in their forties – her age, for God's sake – ostentatiously toting their wriggling infants, which invariably ended up on the knee of some passing female administrator or girl undergraduate. A baby was the new designer accessory, and it came with a whole new set of attitudes. Rupert had been annoying enough as a thoroughly Caucasian critic of post-colonial literature. Now he had become, however briefly, if not a male feminist at least a fellow traveller of feminism, and here he was at a women's studies conference to prove it. His small babe, sleeping sweetly in its baby sling throughout the proceedings, had ensured him a constant flutter of attention from radical sisters not nearly as hard line as they looked.

But it wasn't only Rupert. Despite the success of her paper, Morgan had felt at odds with the whole occasion. Was it that living with Lin, learning her language, had begun to exile Morgan from the fake complexities of academic discourse, or was it simply that Lin had never felt that earnest need to theorise her own experience? Lin, Morgan realised enviously, had never in her life had to listen to six papers in succession on the precursors of Jane Austen, let alone give one.

Thinking, much more cheerfully now, about how she detested Jane Austen, whose narrow range of narrative possibilities still straitjacketed the minds, and indeed the lives, of her female readers, Morgan took the turning which led to the cottage. It was only as she parked the car that she remembered the other baby which ought to have been at the conference, Rosalind's baby.

Rosalind Gilbert was one of Morgan's graduate supervisees, a rather earnest and anxious young woman who seemed haunted by the awareness that her own work, on the passage of time in the novels of Samuel Richardson, paled into insignificance beside that of her husband. Morgan recalled that there was a television programme this weekend about Andrew Gilbert and his brother; she must remember to watch it. And also to give Rosalind a ring sometime and check she was all right. She had an idea that the baby was rather fragile; hadn't it spent its first two months in an incubator?

And wasn't there something else she had promised to do? Trying to remember what it was, Morgan made her way down the overgrown garden towards Lin's painting-shed, the desire she had felt briefly that morning beginning to stir inside her.

CHAPTER TWO

Lin had originally chosen the cottage largely because the ramshackle shed at the bottom of the garden could be turned into a studio. Morgan, gloomily resigned to the fact that living with Lin meant living in the country, had driven as hard a bargain as she could, holding out for plenty of built-in bookshelves and no cats. In the seven years they had lived there, Lin had transformed what had once been an orderly vegetable patch into a flowering wilderness, in which bronze fennel and cream and purple ornamental cabbages mingled with a vigorous and apparently unchecked tangle of garden flowers and decorative weeds under the crabbed old fruit trees which had been there since the cottage was built.

On this particular spring evening, great orange-red tulips glowed in the last of the sunlight among bluebells and cow-parsley and the nettles which Lin encouraged for the sake of eventual butterflies. Morgan threaded her way through the vegetation, avoiding anything which stung or prickled. Inside the shed, she knew, Lin would be staring at the painting on her easel, brush poised, in that trance of concentration in which she was capable of spending the whole of a working day. Lin's painting was the opposite of her gardening; she only painted the bones of things, with a spareness of line and an austere dedication to technique which Morgan found both impressive and disquieting. She sometimes wondered uneasily whether she herself was anything like as important to Lin, during working hours at least, as her latest canvas.

Now she tugged at the clapper of the bell whose vibrations would tell Lin that she was there and pushed open the door. Her bad humour abruptly returned when she saw that Lin was not alone. Standing in front of his own easel, with his sleeves rolled up and a paintbrush in his hand, was Oliver Cresswell. Lin had given him a large piece of cartridge paper pinned to a drawing-board and Ollie had obviously been at work for some time. The paper was covered with a murky dark-green network of trunks and branches. He paid no attention to Morgan's arrival, just went on sloshing in the details of his jungle.

Lin had looked round as Morgan came in. Her silvery hair was tied back, and she wore a paint-spattered man's shirt as a smock. Ollie, Morgan was not pleased to see, was wearing her own pvc apron with the map of the Paris Métro, the one she used for cooking. It would need to be scrubbed before she could use it again.

Irritably she raised her eyebrows at Ollie's painting and signed to Lin, 'Is Daphne saving the rain forest these days?'

Lin signed back, 'Be quiet. You know he has eyes in the back of his head. It's his best painting so far.'

Morgan said loudly, 'So what's this story about Alka-Seltzer, then, Ollie? Collington said he was missing.' She was aware that she had been unable to keep the irritation out of her voice. It was only too easy to dislike Oliver Cresswell, hard as she tried to tell herself that it wasn't the poor little bugger's fault that his mother was bringing him up like that. She found Lin's encouragement of him hard to understand, except as evidence of a nature tolerant almost to the point of saintliness. Even Lin, though, drew the line at Daphne Cresswell.

Oliver's mother had discovered, when her son was barely four, that he had a freak gift for numbers. In the six years since then, she had seen to it that Ollie was coached and coddled and publicised into a precocious little genius. At the age of seven he had featured in the first of several television programmes to be devoted to his talents. At eight he had sat A levels in pure and applied mathematics, achieving full marks and a rash of newspaper headlines. At nine he had finally achieved his mother's goal by taking up a university place. Morgan still ground her teeth over the fact that not only was the university in question the one at which she herself taught but Daphne

Cresswell had then bought a house in the nearest village to the cottage she shared with Lin.

The university had very sensibly insisted that Oliver's degree course must be combined with some normal schooling. Up to that point, Ollie had seldom encountered another child and had certainly never played with one, while his education, apart from maths, had consisted only of astronomy, chess and violin lessons. Reading and writing he had, Daphne claimed, taught himself at a tender age. Daphne had satisfied the university's requirements by enrolling Ollie part-time at the village school, where he must, Morgan supposed, feel a total misfit. It was hard to imagine him joining in the playground games and gossip. He was a silent, self-absorbed little boy, thin and bespectacled and with something chilly about his demeanour, as if constantly aware of being surrounded by his intellectual inferiors.

Morgan couldn't remember how she and Lin had come to be saddled with him. Somehow he had taken to turning up, uninvited and unannounced, at the door of the painting-shed, as persistent as the cat that Morgan had refused to let them have, until Lin had allowed him in. To begin with, he had done tight little drawings of geometric shapes, carefully shaded in black and white. Lin had confiscated his pencil and ruler and provided him with jars of poster paint and enormous brushes, and now he painted large sombre pictures which he refused to take home with him. As far as Morgan could see, he was reassuringly lacking in artistic talent.

While he showed scant evidence of either affection or gratitude, Oliver seemed to regard Lin with the respect due to an equal. He had learned to sign far more easily than Morgan herself had done and would sometimes engage Lin in grave conversation. Morgan, on the other hand, he usually ignored completely. One of the few times Morgan had glimpsed an almost human side to him had been over the choice of his signing name. Lin's was Sky, because of the colour of her eyes. Morgan's was Bird, because of her surname.

Oliver had said firmly, 'I don't want you to call me Professor. Or anything to do with spectacles or that stupid boy wizard. I get enough of that at school.'

Asked what he did want to be called, he had made a sign that even Lin had never seen before.

'What does that mean, Ollie?'

'It's a Kainu hunting-sign. For when they have to be quiet in the forest. Dr Blair-Guthrie showed me. It means a ... I don't know the out-loud name.' His hands sketched a lithe, fast-moving creature. He added in English, 'It's a clan totem, Dr Blair-Guthrie said.' So that was what they called him, without ever discovering if his name-creature was a mammal or a reptile.

Elspeth Blair-Guthrie had adopted Ollie rather as she had adopted Alka-Seltzer. As friendless on campus, where he effortlessly outshone all the other students in his maths seminars, as he was in the primary school playground, Ollie had found his way to Elspeth's flat with the same sort of instinct which had made him attach himself to Lin. They were, Morgan thought, the only two people in the world who never treated him like a sideshow, never used the word gifted about him or gawped at his oddness. Lin simply accepted him as a fellow painter, while Elspeth had seen too wide and too strange a selection of human societies in over sixty years of fieldwork to find anything especially unusual about Ollie.

As for Morgan herself, she was uneasily aware that her own dislike for the child was something he had partly engineered. His cold, strangely adult dismissal of her as wholly without interest was meant to rile her, meant to exclude her from his friendship with Lin. It must be hard, Morgan reminded herself for the hundredth time, being Oliver Cresswell, boy genius.

She said again, more kindly, 'What's happened to Alka-Seltzer, Ollie?'

The child turned round from the easel and began to tell his story not to her but to Lin. While his hands set the scene, his face expressed an urgency Morgan had never seen in him before, as if this tale had been bottled up inside him all day and now was bursting to get out. He plainly believed what he was saying and needed Lin to believe it too This might be fantasy, Morgan thought, but it was not make-believe or attention-seeking. All the same, it couldn't possibly be true. Why would anyone want to kidnap a battered old tomcat like Alka-Seltzer?

CHAPTER THREE

For Oliver, feeding Alka-Seltzer had been a welcome opportunity to escape for a bit from the boredom of the holidays. He had already completed the maths project for next term and while the village kids played kiddish games he wasn't invited to join or tore around on their bikes, he had nothing to do except play chess against himself and practise the violin. If he had had a bike himself he could have gone off on secret expeditions, but his mother wouldn't let him ride one. 'Much too dangerous, Ollie darling,' she always said.

'I could wear a helmet,' Oliver would reply crossly. 'If it's my precious brain-cells you're fussing about again.'

'Now don't be difficult, Ollie. Mummy has already said no. Surely you have some work to do. You mustn't start slacking, darling. You're a university student now, remember.'

She hadn't been any too keen at first on his feeding Alka-Seltzer, either. Oliver had had to argue quite hard to persuade her. In term time, she was the one who ferried him to and fro, something she had no intention of doing for a cat.

'The bus goes right to the campus. I wouldn't have to cross the road, even. Dr Blair-Guthrie will think it's really babyish if I say I can't do it after all. She trusts me even if you don't. I'm not a little kid anymore. I'm a university student now, remember.'

Elspeth's large, dusty flat was full of fascinating and mysterious objects – spears and masks and drums and carved figures decorated with beads or even with human teeth. Her bookshelves were exciting to rummage through. There was over an hour to wait every morning before the next bus back to the village and Oliver made the most of it. Besides, he really liked Alka-Seltzer. He was just what a cat ought to be, tough and self-reliant and not in the least soppy. Alka-Seltzer was a totem animal, Oliver thought, like his own green tree lizard. He was the totem of the campus clan.

That morning, as every morning, he had let himself into the flat with the key that Elspeth had given him. Usually, Alka-Seltzer would be waiting for him in the kitchen, looking reproachfully at his dish. This time he wasn't there. Oliver opened the tin of cat-food and spooned the evil-smelling stuff into the dish. Then he started to go from room to room, searching.

Not in the sitting-room. Not in Elspeth's bedroom. Oliver went down the hallway, his plimsolls making no noise on the worn beige matting. Not in the spare room. Not in the bathroom. Oliver began to feel anxious. He knew that sometimes Alka-Seltzer got into fights and came home wounded.

He called, 'Alk! Alkie! Food time, Alkie! Where are you?' and thought he heard something moving behind the study door. Of course, he thought. Alka-Seltzer liked to sleep on top of the tallboy. Elspeth had even put a cushion up there for him.

Telling the story to Lin, he drew the scene on the air in front of him. Himself opening the door. No Alka-Seltzer on top of the tallboy. No Alka-Seltzer anywhere in the room. The window closed. The cushion lying on the floor. Himself picking up the cushion. Finding it still warm.

Alka-Seltzer could open doors, but he couldn't manage windows. And Oliver knew that he hadn't come out through the door. He had rushed over to the window, just in time to see the car sliding away. A dark blue BMW with two men inside.

'Did you memorise the number?' asked Morgan, intrigued in spite of herself.

'I don't need to memorise numbers,' said Oliver contemptuously.

'Are you sure Alka-Seltzer wasn't sleeping somewhere else in the flat?' asked Lin.

'He wasn't. I checked. I searched everywhere.' Intently, Oliver acted out the thoroughness of his search. 'And then I went and told Collington, but he didn't believe me. So then I got the bus into town and went to the police station.'

It had been a humiliating experience. All his life Oliver had been used to people thinking he was clever. The policeman had thought he was a silly little kid playing at detectives. His kindness as he told Oliver to run along was worse than anger could have been.

Lin and Morgan were not much better. They didn't say they disbelieved him, but he could tell that they didn't really care whether his story was true or not. They weren't going to do anything to get Alka-Seltzer back. Elspeth had trusted him to look after Alka-Seltzer and he had failed There was nothing more he could do. He put down his paintbrush and went home.

It didn't surprise Morgan that Ollie left without saying goodbye. He always did that. But there was something about the set of his shoulders as he walked away which unexpectedly caught her sympathy for a moment. Poor little sprog, she thought vaguely.

CHAPTER FOUR

Morgan sliced a lemon and poured gin over the ice in a couple of tumblers. She felt as if it had been a long day. Lin found the almost-empty tonic bottle and gave it a shake, dissipating the few bubbles that were left.

Morgan said, 'Never mind. I only drink it for the quinine.'

She carried her glass through into the sitting-room and stretched out luxuriously on the sofa, her long legs in their cowboy boots propped on one arm, her head on the other. Lin, still in her paint-streaked smock, came and looked down at her. Morgan placed her glass carefully on the floor.

Her hands said, 'Come here. I want you.'

A wordless and unmeasured time later, Morgan discovered that she was ravenously hungry and sat up. She was surprised to find the room in darkness. Lin, her silvery hair and fair skin glimmering palely in the dusk, began to gather up her clothes and put them on. Placidly, with that abrupt switch into practicality which often overcame her after lovemaking, she pulled the curtains and switched on the light.

'I'll make dinner tonight, Bird. You'll get food on that shirt if you cook.'

This was true enough. Morgan's cooking was fast, furious and creative, and it required the protection of an apron – the apron which Ollie had dropped, smeared with green poster paint, on the studio floor. Lin, on the other hand, cooked with meditative slowness, chopping things thoughtfully into exactly equal bits. Dinner would probably take some time.

Morgan reached for what was left of her gin and switched on the television. Several hours seemed to have unaccountably vanished; no wonder she was hungry. She had completely missed the evening news. The tail end of the weather forecast – a sunny day in most areas with light mist in coastal districts – was followed by a science programme. Watching with only half an eye, her thoughts still preoccupied with Lin, Morgan's attention was unexpectedly caught by a familiar face and voice. She sat up and started to listen with curiosity and interest.

Elspeth Blair-Guthrie was no less striking on the small screen than she was in real life. Her gaunt, freckled face, dominated by an eye like an eagle's and a high, patrician nose, was surmounted by a frizz of white hair, escaping in uncontrolled wisps from the confinement of its bun. As always, she was wearing her ancient and perennial tweed coat and skirt, which looked as if it had once done her sterling service in the jungles of South America. Her voice recalled a vanished age and a vanished caste; the precise tones of an old-fashioned Edinburgh girls' boarding-school overlaying the singing lilt which had distinguished a horde of children who over seventy years ago had run wild on the Highland moorland round a mock-baronial castle.

The film cut to a black and white image of a group of tribesmen, naked except for penis-guards and feather earrings, their bodies elaborately scarified and their faces tattooed with neat parallel lines of dots, swirling elegantly over their cheek-bones. The fierce concentration with which they were attempting to out-stare the camera made them look like the subjects of some nineteenth century photographer. In the midst of them, a white woman who was unmistakably a young Elspeth Blair-Guthrie, her hair dark and her face unwrinkled. The voice-over spoke of Dr Blair-Guthrie's years of fieldwork among the Kainu people, of her discovery of their unique knowledge of healing plants, and of the massacre which, though it had put a stop to her research, had paradoxically led to this belated breakthrough for Western medicine. Elspeth then took up the story again, dryly relating how, after the attack on the tribe, the shaman had given her a necklace of medicinal nuts and seeds to help heal her injuries and how, on her return home, she had donated this to Edinburgh Botanic Garden, where they had managed to get some of the seeds to germinate. Morgan could sense her reluctance to revisit an episode which had put an end to her work with the forest people and left her unable to get about without a stick.

This led into an interview with Andrew Gilbert in his laboratory, describing how his own research had been sparked off when he had attended a lecture by Elspeth on the medicine and magic of the rain forest, during which she had shown a slide of one of these specimens, which had just flowered for the first time. Curiously enough, it was related to the rubber tree. The tribe regarded it as particularly sacred and used it in their coming-of-age ceremonies because of the sperm-like appearance of its viscous sap. He had been interested enough to collaborate on a research paper and then to conduct some practical experiments of his own which had proved unexpectedly successful.

He went on to explain the effects of various extracts of the bark, sap and berries on some soulful-looking monkeys. The work was obviously of the utmost importance, but Andrew's account of its complexities was rather upstaged by the sad-eyed appeal of his experimental subjects. Morgan cursed. The last thing the university needed right now was to have public attention drawn to animal experiments. There had already been trouble last term, when militant students had sprayed the walls of the Biology Building with giant slogans and slightly injured a technician while attempting to break into one of the animal houses.

The voice-over explained that Andrew had been working closely for several years now with his brother, the surgeon James Gilbert. A shot of the brothers together established their identical twinliness. The combination of Andrew's drug with conventional surgery offered hope for the first time of successfully treating children suffering from a rare and hitherto fatal congenital disorder. Laboratory work with rhesus monkeys had yielded very promising results, and James was now ready to apply the treatment to a human patient.

There followed footage of James Gilbert in a children's ward, examining a pallid baby propped up on the lap of a plain, middle-aged woman, the nervous mother replying in whispered monosyllables to the cheery remarks of the surgeon, the voice-over saying that this revolutionary treatment could well mean the difference between life and death for little Ishmael Potter.

Lin's voice called through from the kitchen to tell Morgan that dinner was ready.

The next morning, unusually, Morgan and Lin woke at the same time, the unnaturally early rising that the conference had forced on Morgan corresponding to Lin's idea of a Sunday lie-in. This meant that Morgan, who left to herself would have silenced the alarm clock and stolen another half-hour's sleep, found herself rising in good order and eating a sensible breakfast before setting off for the campus. Perhaps for this reason, perhaps because she had delivered her paper the day before, she found herself in unusually good spirits. It normally took at least until lunchtime for her to get over the shock of having to get out of bed.

The day was as sunny and mild as the weather forecast had promised, with a light haze in the air as she came out on the coast road. Morgan sang to herself tunelessly as she drove. One of the many advantages of living with Lin was the freedom to sing without causing complaint or offence, but it was only alone in the car that Morgan let herself give full rein to her vocal powers. She knew, from many years of lecturing, how to project her voice. It was not until she was approaching the campus that she toned down her joyful rendition of *Climb Every Mountain* to a discreet hum.

As she came out of the carpark she met Rupert Allison, once again accompanied by Joshua in his baby sling. Morgan was feeling sunny enough to greet him with at least the appearance of pleasure. They strolled together towards the Arts Building through the budding and blossoming trees which at this season disguised the functional starkness of the architecture and made the university seem a pleasant place to work.

It was only when they had almost reached their destination that they noticed the police cars. Collington met them in the lobby, his normally impassive face harassed and self-important in more or less equal measure.

'Dr Byrd, miss. Dr Allison, sir. The police are wanting to see everyone who was on campus yesterday afternoon. They've taken over the Senior Common Room for their investigations, if you could just make your way there, sir. Miss.'

Morgan and Rupert glanced at one another, equally perplexed, then Rupert said, 'For heaven's sake, Collington, what on earth is going on?'

Collington's look of self-importance increased and his voice took on a treacly tone, as if it gave him a perverse kind of pleasure to break the bad tidings.

'I would have thought as you'd have heard it on the news last night, sir. It's the Gilbert baby. Seems as though the poor little mite has been kidnapped.'

CHAPTER FIVE

Rupert turned pale. With a curious mixture of sympathy and *schadenfreude,* Morgan saw him clasp the pendant Joshua to his chest, one hand protectively cupping the baby's head. She found that she was blenching herself at the thought of Rosalind's anguish which, as graduate supervisor, it would be her business to try to assuage. Absurdly, she found herself remembering Ollie's defeated shoulders as he walked off through the garden yesterday evening, grieving for the loss of Alka-Seltzer. Hostages to fortune, she thought. It was a great mistake to love anything that much. The thought of Lin flickered through her mind and she dismissed it hastily. Meekly she followed Rupert towards the SCR.

She gave her name and status to the uniformed policeman at the door and was told to take a seat and await her turn to be questioned. The first thing she saw when she entered the room was Rosalind Gilbert, sitting white-faced and tense in a corner and holding Persephone Jane in her arms with the same defensive clutch with which Rupert was holding Joshua.

31

Morgan's double-take was followed by a shameful feeling of relief. The Gilbert baby that Collington had been talking about was not Rosalind's Persephone but James and Libby's Benjamin, and mercifully no business of Morgan's.

As if to hide these thoughts, even from herself, under an appearance of concern, she went over and sat down beside Rosalind, who gave her a pale and nervous smile. Looking round the room, Morgan saw that most of the participants in the early feminist fiction conference were waiting to be interviewed, along with a handful of graduate students and a pair of visiting scholars from Japan. Since it was both the vacation and a weekend, there had been very few people on campus the previous day.

She murmured to Rosalind, 'Can you tell me what's happened, Ros? I've only just heard that Ben is missing.'

Rosalind's hands began to tremble against the shawled bundle of her daughter. She said, 'It's so awful. Poor, poor Libby. If it had been Zeffie ...' She bent her head over the child, apparently close to tears.

Her concern, Morgan noted wryly, was just as self-centred as Rupert's had been. Or her own, for that matter. She was in no position to throw stones at Rosalind.

Gently she asked again, 'Can you tell me what happened?'

The story which Rosalind sketched for her in a halting whisper was essentially the one that Morgan was later to read on the front pages of both the local paper and the *Guardian*. Libby Gilbert had gone up to London on Saturday morning to see her husband, who had operated the previous day on the child that he and Andrew were testing out their theories on and would have to remain on call until the results of the operation became clear. She was only to be away for a few hours and had left Melanie Wilson babysitting Ben.

Morgan's heart sank again at this point. She wasn't off the hook after all. Melanie was an English Department undergraduate, a pale and nervous girl, lank haired and anorexically thin, who found speaking up in seminars virtually impossible though she wrote long, obsessively conscientious essays. She didn't seem to have a home to go to and usually spent the vacations working as a waitress in a local café. It seemed that she had done some babysitting for Rosalind, who had recommended her to Libby after Ben was born. This vacation, with James having to spend nearly all his time between the hospital and his London flat, the Gilberts had taken her on as a sort of *au pair*.

Libby had returned home at the end of the afternoon to find the house in order and Melanie peacefully reading a magazine. Melanie had offered to make her a cup of tea and Libby had sat for some time at the kitchen table, easing off her smart London shoes and chatting about her day, unaware that anything was wrong.

It was only when Melanie said, 'I'll fetch Ben in now, Mrs Gilbert. It's nearly time for his bath,' that either of them realised that the pram was missing.

Benjamin Gilbert had spent the afternoon in the garden under the dappled shade of the maple tree, squinting up at the sparkling bits of sky between the leaves and waving ineffectual hands at the string of brightly coloured beads stretched across the body of his pram. Melanie had, she tearfully insisted, checked him every half hour. She thought the last time must have been just before five o'clock, when she had exchanged a few words over the fence with the woman next door who was taking in her washing. Libby had arrived home at about a quarter past, and the disappearance of both baby and pram was discovered some twenty minutes later. There had been perhaps three quarters of an hour, between roughly ten to five and exactly thirty-seven minutes past, when Libby phoned the police, in which Ben could have been taken.

Rosalind herself had passed her brother and sister-in-law's house in the late afternoon, wheeling Zeffie, and had no recollection of seeing Ben's pram in the garden. However, she could not be certain of the exact time or indeed of whether the pram had actually been missing. She was quite sure, though, that Libby had not yet returned from London. If she had seen the car outside, she would have dropped in for a few minutes.

She had been absent from the conference yesterday because Zeffie, who was getting over a cold, had been fractious and miserable, and she had not wanted either to leave her with a babysitter or to let her grizzling disrupt the proceedings. Like Morgan, she had not heard about the kidnapping until this morning. She had gone to bed early last night and had switched off the phone; Zeffie had kept her up the night before and she had been worn out. A phone-call from Libby at breakfast-time had been followed by one from the police, asking her to come in if she had anything to report. She hoped they would take her story soon and let her go. She wasn't sure how much longer she could keep Zeffie quiet.

Morgan suggested that giving the child a pinch and starting her wailing might be the quickest way of getting out of there, but Rosalind looked shocked at the very idea.

'Oh, I couldn't possibly do a thing like that.'

She repeated miserably how sorry she felt for Libby. She herself was alone in the house at the moment. Andrew was in South America – something to do with his wonder drug – and the very thought that Zeffie might have been kidnapped ...

Morgan was on the point of asking why on earth she should have been, but bit the question back and found a kinder way of putting it.

'You surely don't think that Zeffie was in any danger, do you, Ros? I mean, isn't it usually women who've lost their own babies who steal other people's on impulse? I'm sure they'll find Ben safe and sound in a day or two.'

'There have been threats, you know,' said Rosalind nervously. 'Letters and abusive texts about Andrew's animal work. What if one of these animal rights groups has taken Benjie by mistake?'

Morgan privately thought it pretty unlikely, but said soothingly that she was sure the police would follow it up.

When Morgan's own turn came to be questioned, she gazed blankly at the slightly blurred photograph of Ben Gilbert in his pram and tried to think of something helpful. She recognised the pram, a dark-blue canvas carry-cot on a detachable wheeled undercarriage, but only because Rosalind had a similar one for Zeffie. Ben himself looked to her much the way all small babies did, his starfish hands more distinctive than his anonymous pink blob of a face.

The early feminist fiction conference had ended at five o'clock and her drive home had taken her past the Gilberts' house, but she had noticed nothing suspicious. But then, although she didn't say so, Morgan would have been unlikely to notice a whole procession of nursemaids all of them wheeling prams. Babies were just not her scene. She was, however, able to assure the detective sergeant that Melanie Wilson, at least as far as her university studies were concerned, had shown herself to be diligent to a fault. As far as Morgan knew, she was a completely truthful and reliable person, if a bit over-anxious and only too likely to blame herself for Ben's disappearance.

It was becoming evident, by the time Morgan had given her statement, that the rest of the conference would have to be abandoned. It had only been scheduled to last until lunchtime anyway, and half the morning was already gone. Morgan felt secretly relieved to be able to remove herself with a clear conscience. She drove into town to buy a Sunday paper but found that, despite being mentioned on the local news the night before, Ben's kidnapping had not yet been picked up by the national press. It would doubtless be all over the front pages by tomorrow, though.

Morgan found that she didn't want to go back to the cottage, where Lin, she knew, would be engrossed in her morning's work and reluctant to be disturbed. Instead she drove along the sea road and parked by a deserted stretch of shingle. She walked gloomily across the crunchy expanse of the beach, lobbing pebbles into the water and thinking about Melanie, who must be hysterical with distress, and about what might be happening to Ben, and about her own total lack of maternal instinct.

When she and Lin had started living together, she had been amazed to find that several of her straight women friends assumed that they were intending to have artificial insemination and bring up the resultant offspring as one big happy family.

One of them had even asked whether Lin had a brother, as the most suitable father for Morgan's child. She had thought at the time, and still did, that they were all completely crazy. It was Lin she wanted to live with, not a wailing brat who shared some of Lin's genes. In any case, she could never think of anything to say to babies.

It left her unable to imagine what Libby Gilbert must be going through now. Or the mother of that child that James Gilbert had operated on the day before yesterday. She found she didn't even want to imagine. With a shiver as if someone had just walked across her grave, Morgan rammed her balled fists into her jacket pockets and strode on across the shifting pebbles of the beach.

CHAPTER SIX

While Morgan walked gloomily along the shore, thinking about the unimaginable nature of human loss, Libby Gilbert was phoning her husband. Sister Maxwell, listening to one half of the conversation from outside the consulting room door, thought it rather inconsiderate of her.

James Gilbert, his face haggard from lack of sleep, was repeating at intervals, with a patience that was rapidly turning to weariness, 'I'm sorry, darling, but I can't. You must realise that I can't. I know it's terrible for you having to go through this on your own, but I simply can't leave the hospital right now.'

'Look, we have to leave it to the police, darling. If there was anything practical I could do, it would be different. But there isn't. And I'm needed here.'

And then, with the beginnings of anger, 'For God's sake, Libby, I'm not just conducting a medical experiment here, you know. We're talking about a baby. Like Ben. Potentially, a lot of babies like Ben.'

'Well, you try telling that to his mother.'

'Look, I really can't discuss this now.'

'All right, it may be unfeeling but it's my job. You knew all that when you married me. It isn't any different just because Ben ...'

'Look, I didn't mean it like that. Of course I'm worried about him. Terribly worried. I'm worried about both of you.'

'I'm sorry, but I have to go now, darling. I'll phone you this evening. I love you.'

He put down the phone and rubbed his hands over his face as if to wipe the conversation from his mind. Libby was right – he was unfeeling. He could feel nothing at all, only an immense emptiness into which not only his son but his wife had vanished. All he wanted to do was get on with the day's work as if nothing had happened. Jesus Christ, as if nothing had happened.

Sister Maxwell knocked discreetly, then poked her head round the edge of the door, concern mixed with curiosity written too plainly on her face. She had known him a long time. James Gilbert rolled up his shirt sleeves, picked up his case notes and put them down again. He sighed.

'Look, Maxie,' he said, 'don't spread this around yet, but someone has taken Ben.' He swallowed, and went on with more difficulty. 'My son. Someone has kidnapped him. It's probably just some poor woman desperate for a baby, and the police will catch up with her in no time. Oxbourne is quite a small place, after all. They're bound to find him.' He sounded dogmatic about it, as if he was trying to convince Sister Maxwell of something she was obstinately refusing to grasp. 'Anyway, it'll be in all the papers tomorrow, and I don't want gossip. Anyone talking to the press. I shall be getting on with my work as usual and I expect everyone else in the unit to do the same. Is that clear?' He glared at her, daring her to utter a word of sympathy.

She said, in a voice like a nanny's, 'I've never had any gossip on my ward, and I don't intend to start now.' She smoothed down her pale blue tunic fiercely at the very idea, then glanced at the fob watch clipped to its pocket. 'The Johnson baby is poorly this morning, but Baby Potter is holding his own nicely. Mother seems a bit anxious though. I think you should have a word with her.'

The bare white room held five transparent-sided cots. In each one lay a sickly baby, its tiny body hooked up to tubes and monitors. There was the steady hum of high-tech equipment, the occasional thin whimper of a child, the brisk footsteps of nurses. By two of the cots, young mothers in sweatshirts and leggings held the hands of nervous lads whose first experience of fatherhood had plunged them into a nightmare. By the third, a pair of earnest middle-class parents were trying to build a therapeutic relationship between two small boys in school uniform and the baby sister they were soon to lose. The fourth cot had no one sitting by it. Police and social workers were still trying to determine which of the parents was responsible for the state of the infant inside.

The woman by the fifth cot was oblivious to all this. She was sitting, as she had been doing now for several hours, gazing intently at the inert body of her son. She was holding a Bible on her knee, open at the passage that had been vouchsafed to her earlier that morning when she had taken up the Book, seeking for guidance. Her lips moved, repeating soundlessly over and over the words she had been led to: 'Call me not Naomi, call me Mara: for the Almighty hath dealt very bitterly with me. I went out full, and the Lord hath brought me home again empty.'

James Gilbert, coming into the ward under the respectful escort of Sister Maxwell, realised after one glance why Sister was more worried about the mother than the baby. That fixed white stare and those silently moving lips suggested a degree of distress unusual even in that room. He recollected that this was Mrs Potter's only child, and that she herself was nearer fifty than forty. But the operation had gone well and the short-term prognosis, at least, was good. And if the work that he and Andrew had been doing was as valuable as they now believed it to be, there was a better than evens chance of a complete recovery.

He began his round, as always, with the incubator nearest the door, leaving Mrs Potter to be dealt with last. The Morrison baby was doing well. The parents should be able to take her home in about ten days' time. The Taylor baby would be going into theatre tomorrow; he should pull through, with luck. The Johnson baby was unlikely to last the week. The smaller of her two brothers told him chattily, 'We're telling our baby goodbye,' making his parents smile at him with sorrowful pride. The larger boy said nothing and twisted his hands together shyly. His eyes were furtive, as if he had understood too much.

James heard himself saying all the usual things as he examined each child and attempted to support or reassure the parents. His voice sounded completely false to him, its tone of confident professional benevolence a plummy sham, but the parents didn't seem to notice. Perhaps they expected a consultant to sound like that.

The Cairns baby offered a respite from talking, but the sight of her injuries almost cracked his defences. Desperately, he wrenched his mind away from the thought of what might be happening, might already have happened, to Ben and brought it back to the small, brutalised body in the cot. The fractured ribs were mending but it was still too early to assess the full

43

extent of the brain damage. He murmured to Sister, made a note on his file and moved on to the Potter baby.

Under different circumstances, his main emotions would have been pride in his own skill and excitement at the potential medical breakthrough that this case represented, but the loss of Ben, combined with Mrs Potter's obvious distress, had changed all that. The mother did not relax her strained attention on the child until Sister Maxwell gently tapped her on the shoulder.

'Here's Mr Gilbert come to look at baby, dear.'

She looked up then and met James's eye with a gaze which seemed to go beyond him into some private hell. She said, 'I've been pondering in my mind if I've done right.'

James said heartily, 'I know it's early days yet, but Isaac is making splendid progress so far, Mrs Potter.'

Mrs Potter's haunted gaze did not waver. She said tonelessly, 'Ishmael. We call him Ishmael.'

James wondered about that 'we'. There had been no sign of a Mr Potter. As far as he knew, the poor woman was alone in the world apart from Elspeth Blair-Guthrie.

'Yes, of course. Ishmael. I know it's distressing for you to see him in discomfort like this, but he really does have a good chance of recovery.'

'Perhaps it wasn't meant.'

James's eye fell on the book she was holding. The consolations of religion didn't seem to be doing very much for Mrs Potter. For himself, he found it impossible to conceive of a God who would let what had happened to the Cairns baby ... He blotted out the thought before it led him to Ben.

He said, 'You've done the best you could for your child, Mrs Potter. Now, I just want to take a look at him to see how he's doing.'

In the same toneless voice she repeated, 'Perhaps it wasn't meant.'

Sister Maxwell took over with practised smoothness. 'Nonsense, dear. It's time you had some rest. It won't help baby if you make yourself ill. We'll make sure he's all right. That's what we're here for. Now, we'll just get you tucked up in bed and give you something to make you sleep.'

Mrs Potter gave no sign of having understood but she reacted automatically to the no-nonsense, infantilising tone, rising obediently to her feet and letting herself be led away.

Libby Gilbert came back into the kitchen with clenched fists and flushed cheeks. Her throat dry with anger, she said, 'All he cares about is that bloody hospital. He wouldn't care if Ben was ...' She broke off in horror at having so nearly uttered the unsayable, unthinkable word.

Octavia said firmly, 'Sit down, Libby. I'll put the kettle on.'

'All I've had since it happened is bloody cups of tea. Everyone's behaving as if it was the Blitz.'

WPC Davis said stolidly, 'Well, I could do with a cup, anyway, Mrs Castlemain.'

Libby, defeated, subsided into a chair. Octavia pushed the biscuit tin towards her.

'Where's Melanie?'

'Upstairs in her room. She won't stop crying.'

'You've enough on your plate without that. She can come back with me when I go to fetch my overnight bag. I'll tell her I need someone to look after Dick and the boys.'

Octavia Castlemain was a manager. A lifetime of benevolent despotism had taught her that the secret of power is relentless delegation. She not only did good works, she was the cause of good works in others. She ran the Oxfam shop, the parent-teacher association and the local branch of the Woodcraft Folk, and now she was managing Libby. As soon as she heard about Ben, she had turned up carrying a large tin of home-baked biscuits and calmly made it plain that she would be staying the night. Like most people, Libby had always found Octavia's bossiness a bit of a joke. Now the thought of being rid of Melanie's incessant weeping filled her with gratitude, though she felt honour-bound to make a feeble protest on behalf of Richard, Octavia's silent and long-suffering husband.

'Dick and the boys won't want to listen to her crying either.'

'The boys won't mind. They're at the age when they think that all girls do is cry. And Dick will hardly notice.'

'Well, if you're sure it won't be a nuisance. Tell Dick she doesn't eat meat. Or fish either, come to that.'

'Not to worry. She can survive for a few days on baked beans and macaroni cheese.'

'She only eats vegetarian cheese,' said Libby despondently. 'Though she doesn't eat much of anything really.'

'She won't starve,' said Octavia comfortably. 'Don't fuss about it, Libby.'

As if she were continuing with a subject that had not been broken off, Libby said, 'I just feel so angry with him, Octavia. There's this child at the hospital, he's Ben's age. James operated on him on Friday and he's still in intensive care. God, Friday seems such a long time ago. And I know James has to stay there. I know he does. But I just feel so angry. I feel how dare he put this child before Ben.'

Octavia said placidly, 'Men find it so hard to face up to their feelings. They take refuge in their work instead.'

'And I feel so helpless just sitting here,' said Libby desperately. 'If only there was something I could do.'

WPC Davis said, 'We're pulling out all the stops to find him, Mrs Gilbert. If he's still missing tomorrow, you'll be making that television appeal.'

'What about posters?' said Octavia. She was famous for her posters; they had advertised a host of worthy causes.

'We might consider that if it turns into a long-term investigation, but at this stage we're still hoping that won't happen.'

'No, I was thinking of getting on and making them now. The police wouldn't have any objections?'

'I suppose not,' said WPC Davis doubtfully.

'Right, that's settled then,' said Octavia, snapping briskly into organising mode. 'Get your laptop, Libby. And we'll need a good photo of Ben. That one on the dresser will do. The office printer's in Oxbourne opens early. I'll get them to run us off a couple of hundred to start with, the largest size they do. Then we'll have to decide how widely to spread them. I'll phone the Woodcraft mums this evening and rope them in to help with the driving.'

Dazed by all this bustle after the endless-seeming hours of inactivity, Libby fetched the laptop and took the framed photograph of Ben off the dresser. Between the dark blue hood of the pram and the multi-coloured string of beads, his smiling face looked out at her, infinitely familiar and dear. She dared not let herself wonder if she would ever see it again. She turned the frame over and began to prise off the back. At the kitchen table, Octavia was typing HAVE YOU SEEN THIS CHILD?

CHAPTER SEVEN

In a hotel room in San Lorenzo, Elspeth Blair-Guthrie was also looking at a photograph. Outside the window, in the deeply shadowed canyons between the raw cliffs of skyscrapers, the early morning traffic was already adding its emissions to the fog of pollution which hung deceptively over the city like summer haze in the early morning light. Hard to believe that here too the unchanging forest had once spread its green canopy. It was of the forest and its people that Elspeth was thinking as she gazed with unseeing eyes at the image of Oliver Cresswell. Of the forest people, and of this boy whose fate she had chosen to link with theirs.

In the decades since her time with the Kainu, Elspeth had become convinced of the harmfulness of European contact with the rain forest people, and she had always been concerned about the exploitation of their tribal knowledge. Though she had published descriptions of Kainu medical practices in *Ritual and Reality*, the book that had made her name as an anthropologist back in the 1960s, she had not included any information that the tribe regarded as sacred. She was not to know that over half a century later Andrew Gilbert would need that information to speed up his research into a possible cure for Beaufort-Lindgren's disease – rare in the general population, but rife in the local community she had gone on to study, the little Christian sect called the Sealed Brethren.

She returned her attention to the photograph. Oliver Cresswell's proud, impassive face wore the same look that she had seen so many times, in the forest, on the faces of boys on the threshold of initiation. Had she been wrong to put that look on Oliver's face? Was she endangering him by involving him in the intrigues and corruption of an alien world? Would he, if the need arose, be equal to the task that she had laid on his narrow shoulders?

She remembered the conversation with which it had all begun. Oliver, cross and frustrated, was sitting on the battered old sofa in her study, gently teasing Alka-Seltzer's ears to make them twitch.

'It's not fair,' he was saying indignantly. 'I get held back all the time because the other students are so thick, and then they all just go off to the snack bar without me. As if I didn't belong. And at school it's even worse. The stupid little kids have stupid little gangs and they leave me out. And at home there's only my mother and she just treats me like a baby. I wish I was grown-up *now*. I hate being ten.'

'In some cultures, that's the age at which boys become men,' said Elspeth.

'What cultures?' Oliver asked gloomily. 'I wish I belonged to one of them.'

Elspeth stared at him, the plan suddenly whole and entire in her head.

'Can you keep a secret, Oliver?'

'Of course I can.'

'No, think about it first. It's important.'

Coming from anyone but Elspeth, Oliver would have taken that as an insult. Under Elspeth's austere, eagle gaze he considered the matter seriously. *Had* he ever kept a secret, a big one? He kept little secrets from his mother all the time, of course, but those didn't count. Perhaps his only true secret was not really being who he seemed to be, and that one he shared with Elspeth and Lin. But already he could see that having a proper grown-up secret, an important one, would be both a shield and a weapon for that hidden self. It was something he had needed for a long time without knowing it.

'Yes,' he said soberly at last, 'I think so.'

'You said the kids at your school have gangs. A tribe is more important than a gang. How would you like to become a man of the Kainu people?'

'I don't like games,' said Oliver suspiciously.

'This isn't a game. It's real and it's secret and it might even be dangerous.'

'OK then.'

'You'll have to be prepared to learn a lot of difficult things. A new language, a new way of thinking, a new identity even.'

'That's all right,' said Oliver. 'Learning's what I'm best at.'

This had indeed proved to be true. She had coached Oliver intensively for several months and he had learned almost as rapidly as a boy of the tribe would have done. And now she was back in this land she had never expected to return to. As it turned out, she had not even had to invent a pretext for her journey. The international conference on the future of tribal peoples was being held in San Lorenzo as part of General Paragual's attempt to demonstrate to the world, and especially to the United States government, that his regime would be different from that of his predecessor. Elspeth disliked lending her name and reputation to this charade, but the conference gave her the chance to meet openly with the human rights lawyer Ramón Perez and even enabled her to bring Andrew Gilbert with her, under the cover of presenting a paper on biodiversity and modern medicine.

While Elspeth had felt some compunction about involving Oliver in her plans, she felt none whatever about blackmailing Andrew. She could hardly blame him for exploiting the botanical knowledge of the Kainu, given that both the information and the plant material were only in the public domain because she herself had put them there, but having meddled in the first place, she felt an obligation to try to secure some financial recompense for the tribe. In any case, Andrew had earlier had no compunction about blackmailing her. Sacred meant secret to the Kainu, and there were details about the uses of the nau tree which she had been careful to omit from her book. It was Andrew who had extracted those details, trading them not just against the cost in dead monkeys of letting him discover through his own experiments what she already knew but also, potentially, against the life of Naomi Potter's child. She was aware that in return she had stooped to rather underhand tactics, but needs must when the devil drives.

'Your private life is your own affair, Andrew, of course, but you would not have developed this drug without my assistance. Before young people became so dismally conformist, they used to say that property is theft. If it were merely a matter of my own intellectual property, I might be inclined to agree, but in this case, I'm as much of a thief as you. So given the deal you are intending to make with Gifford Pharmaceuticals, not to mention your other plans, I think it would be a good thing if you came with me to San Lorenzo.' She had fixed him with a steely eye and added unconvincingly, 'Anyway, dear boy, I'm an old woman now and my wretched leg is such a nuisance. I could do with some assistance on the journey.'

Ramón Perez would be arriving shortly to drive her and Andrew to the arranged meeting-place in a town near the mountains. Elspeth sighed, thinking of this. She would have liked to see the forest once again before she died, but Ramón had been right not to risk it. Even as it was, they were taking risks enough. She became aware that she was still holding Oliver's photograph and scrutinised it for a moment with narrowed eyes before nodding as if something had been decided between them and putting it carefully into her capacious handbag.

Meanwhile, in the small town of Mercedes, two hundred miles into the interior, Father Miguel Hernández was buying a black cock. The brown-skinned old woman who kept the market stall handed it over to him crammed roughly into a string bag, struggling and pecking as fiercely as if it already knew its fate. Father Hernández took hold of it gingerly by its trussed and scaly feet. He had flown in from the mission station the day before with Aapuulo the chief, two of the tribal elders and the shaman, plus the eleven-year-old boy who would act as proxy in the ritual. Though he had managed to kit them out for the trip with ill-fitting European clothes, it still seemed better that none of them should be seen in the streets. All the same, it troubled him to be involved in the preparations for the ceremony.

In over half a century of working with the Kainu, Father Hernández had cured many of them but converted none. He knew that behind his back they called him Meru-ra, which means 'the mistaken one', a kindly way of referring to those a little touched in the head, but they respected his medical knowledge as he respected theirs. The Kainu children were not baptised but at least they were all inoculated. Now he had been drawn into assisting in what he instinctively felt to be an act of blasphemy. He would have crossed himself, but he needed both hands to control the struggling bird. He murmured under his breath, 'Santa María, Madre de Dios, it is for the sake of the tribe. Make your Son to understand that it is for the sake of the tribe.'

The cock was the last thing to be bought. In a basket over one arm, Father Hernández was already carrying the rest of his purchases, the incense, the sweet herbs, the bottle of spirits. The shaman had brought the sacred knives and the manhood beads from the forest, along with other items that Father Hernández preferred not to know about. Elspeth Blair-Guthrie would be bringing the only other thing that was needed for the ceremony. She would be here in an hour or two and the thought of seeing his old friend again after so many years was as much a sorrow as a joy to Father Hernández.

It brought back too vividly the night of the massacre, that night when he had delivered Aapuulo's grandmother of a boy child, hiding in the forest, the sky reddened by the light of the burning huts, the dying woman willing herself to survive long enough for her baby to be born and not to cry out so that the soldiers should not find them.

That child's son was now chief in his father's place, and he himself was an old man as Elspeth must now be an old woman. A lame old woman, permanently crippled by the events of that distant night. Now, after all these years, they were to be brought together again in the attempt to avert a fresh danger from the tribe. Father Hernández strode on through the colourful bustle of the market, oblivious to it, his lips moving in a prayer which would have astonished his bishop. 'Santa María,' he murmured, 'bless the boy who today becomes a man. Cleanse him and the tribe from the sin which attends his coming to manhood. Let him be a strong shield for his people.' The black cock gave a strangled cry inside the confining net, like a fierce and unsanctified amen.

CHAPTER EIGHT

One of the first results of Octavia's poster campaign was a much-resented loss of freedom of movement for all children living within twenty-five miles of Oxbourne. Mothers of babies would in any case have been following police advice to keep a close eye on them, especially after Libby's movingly self-controlled television appeal to the kidnapper to return Ben to his parents. After the posters went up, even ten-year-olds like Oliver found that the last few days of the Easter holidays would be spent under non-stop supervision.

The mothers of Freshley village organised a rota, and any child who wanted to go out to play was obliged to do so in the boring recreation ground, or in the school hall if wet, under an attentive adult eye. For Oliver, who had private business of his own to see to, having to hang around with a bunch of kids on a patch of scuffed grass with a slide and a row of iron swings was an intolerable frustration. And indeed, nearly all the other children seemed to feel the same way, judging by their grumbles. Derek, Tim and Jason were building a gang den. The Harris twins wanted to go swimming. Cathy and Stephanie, an inseparable pair who were always self-importantly hugging some secret or other, were whispering between themselves about a mysterious game called Black Bag which couldn't be played in the recreation ground.

Oliver had no sense of fellow feeling as he overheard these complaints. It was all kids' stuff, while he himself would soon be a man and had serious preparations to make. And besides, he had to look for Alka-Seltzer. He still really believed the men in the blue BMW had taken him, but if the grown-ups were right and he had just imagined the kidnapping, then Alkie might be lying wounded somewhere. Freshley was much nearer the university by cat-tracks than it was by road and Alka-Seltzer controlled a large territory, but Oliver had already searched the village and its surroundings and found nothing. Today he had intended to look in Hangman's Wood. It was one of his own special places and he had once seen Alka-Seltzer hunting there. And instead, he was stuck in a kiddies' playground. He couldn't even go back home because his mother had gone shopping in Oxbourne and would have locked the door before she left. Oliver sighed deeply, sat down with his back to the fence and pulled out a book.

He wasn't even left to read in peace, though. Fat, dough-faced Mrs Harris, with her smell of scented sweat, came and loomed over him.

'Reading on a nice day like this, dear?'

Since it was perfectly obvious what he was doing, Oliver said nothing.

'Don't you want to come and play a game?'

This time she had at least asked a real rather than a rhetorical question, so without raising his eyes from the page, Oliver said, 'No.' It didn't occur to him to add a thank you, but then it never did.

Thinking what an unlikeable child he was, and no wonder the others wouldn't play with him, Mrs Harris persisted. 'What are you reading, dear? I can see you're nearly at the end. Is it an exciting story?'

Oliver scrambled to his feet and closed the book. It was Stephen Hawking's *The Theory of Everything*.

He said 'I've read it before actually. And actually I think I'll go home now.'

'Oh, I don't think ...'

'I live just over there,' said Oliver contemptuously. 'You can watch till I'm through the front gate if you want.'

He stalked off without a goodbye. Mrs Harris, mindful of her responsibilities, made sure that he did indeed go through the white-painted gate and then turned back thankfully to organise a game of rounders with the others.

Once safely inside the garden and hidden by its hedge, Oliver skirted round the house and made for the gap where the cats had their tunnel. He looked round cautiously before squeezing through. Any grown-up he encountered would be only too likely to send him back to the recreation ground. The coast was clear, however. Walking purposefully and not too fast, to minimise the risk of being stopped and turned back, Oliver set out on his mission.

Hangman's Wood, when he reached it, was thick with new growth. If it wasn't really like the rain forest that Elspeth had described to him, it was still an excellent place to practise forest skills. Oliver moved through the undergrowth like a hunter, careful where he planted his plimsolls. It was hard not to reveal his tracks by bruising the juicy leaves and stems of bluebells. He tried to give the Kainu names that Elspeth had taught him to the creatures that he saw. A jay could well be a parakeet and a grey squirrel a spider monkey. He didn't see anything which corresponded to a green tree lizard, but he repeated the word to himself all the same. He was one of the brothers of the green tree lizard moving stealthily through the forest in search of the great cat totem of the campus clan.

Morgan was sitting in front of her laptop, staring hopefully at her seventh rearrangement of a tricky paragraph, when she heard a banging at the front door. She swore quietly but with conviction as she got up to see who it was. Lin was in

London seeing a gallery owner and Morgan had intended to put in a good day's work on the article on Mary Wollstonecraft which she ought to have finished by the end of the Christmas vacation. It had taken her until mid-afternoon to work up the adrenaline to get started and over an hour to write half a page and now she had visitors.

She was not best pleased when she found Oliver Cresswell on the doorstep. He was panting as if he had been running and had a rather wild-eyed expression on his usually expressionless face.

He said urgently, 'Is Lin here?'

'She's in London,' said Morgan, in a discouraging tone of voice.

'Well, can I come in and use your phone?'

'I'm afraid not,' said Morgan firmly. 'I'm busy.'

'Oh,' said Ollie, disconcerted. 'Only you see I've found a pram.'

'Christ, Ollie, you don't mean ...?'

'In Hangman's Wood,' said Ollie breathlessly. 'And there was something inside it, sort of wrapped in a blanket. So I thought I ought to tell the police and you were the nearest person with a phone. Only it might be better if you told them for me. They didn't believe me the last time.'

'Come in,' said Morgan shortly. 'I'll ring them.'

When the police car arrived, Morgan found herself being addressed as Mrs Burns and asked if she would kindly accompany her son to show them the alleged evidence. It didn't seem a moment for nit-picking accuracy so she just got into the back of the car with Ollie. As they drove, the one who had introduced himself as Detective Chief Inspector Burdock questioned Ollie about his find in a carefully casual voice.

'Can you tell me how you came across it, sonny?'

'I was just walking along through the wood and I came to a sort of clearing and there it was.'

'Did you touch anything?'

'Of course not,' said Oliver indignantly, his pride stung by the suggestion.

'Sure you can find it again?'

'I left patrins.'

'Come again?'

'Tracking signs. You know – crossed twigs and knots of grass.'

'Oh, right. In the cub scouts, are you, sonny?'

'No, I'm not actually.'

Morgan could tell from Ollie's air of contained excitement that he was quite untouched by the feeling of dread which was gripping all three of the adults in the car. Despite his famous brains, at this moment he was just a small boy enjoying the importance of having found a vital clue. He was too young for his imagination to be troubled by the thought of something wrapped in a blanket, something which might well be a dead baby.

Once inside the wood, Ollie led the way with confident certainty, glancing around to find the markers he had left. The place was just as he had described it, a small clearing among the trees with a dark blue pram standing in the middle of an area of crushed and trampled grass and wild flowers. Inspector Burdock caught Morgan's eye and she put a hand on Ollie's reluctant shoulder and led him back a little way among the trees.

Ollie, agonised with curiosity, said, 'But I want to see what they find.'

I don't thought Morgan, feeling herself sweating with the horror of suspense. And then they heard the voice of the sergeant, loud with shock and disbelief.

'Jesus Christ, it's a bleeding cat!'

Oliver tore himself away from Morgan's grasp and dashed back into the clearing. She sprinted after him, in time to see him reach the side of the pram. His voice rose in a shrill cry like that of a much younger child.

'It's Alka-Seltzer! It's Alka-Seltzer! It's all your fault! I told you and you wouldn't listen, and now he's dead.'

She went over and looked down at the unwrapped bundle. Alka-Seltzer was lying among the folds of a blue cellular cot blanket. His body had been stuffed into a yellow Babygro, out of which his head, the glassy eyes still open, lolled at an unnatural angle. Like the sergeant, she was shocked by the grotesqueness of the sight and by its horrible implications. As she stared, cold with terror for the missing child, Ollie suddenly buried his face in the crook of a shielding arm and burst into loud and passionate sobs.

Inspector Burdock drove them back to the cottage, leaving Sergeant Crewe standing guard by the pram until the forensic team arrived. Morgan made tea, stirring several spoonfuls of sugar into Ollie's mug. His tears had stopped but he was still white-faced and rigid with a mixture of anger and grief.

Inspector Burdock took out his notebook. 'OK, sonny, I gather you can identify the deceased for us. That will be a great help with our inquiries. So let's begin with your name, shall we?'

'It's Oliver. Oliver Cresswell.'

Ollie was used to people recognising his name, but the inspector's double-take was nothing to do with having seen him on TV.

'Cresswell? I suppose you realise you're a missing person, lad? Your mother phoned in a couple of hours ago to report you'd gone AWOL. You want to get on the blower right now and tell her you're OK.'

Morgan took one look at his face and said, 'It's all right, Ollie. I'll do it.'

She could see that listening to her telling Daphne about the discovery of Alka-Seltzer's corpse was more than he could have coped with right then, so she slid tactfully out into the passage. She wasn't too sure she could cope with passing on the news herself, nor indeed of how much she ought to say; but in the event that problem solved itself.

Her cautious opener – 'I'm just ringing to let you know that I've got Ollie here; I gather you've been worried' – elicited a gushing and histrionic account of Daphne's anxiety both about the whereabouts and safety of her child and about the bridge party he had nearly made her miss. It was impossible for Morgan to insert a word in edgeways and she sensibly didn't try.

'You simply don't know what it is to be a mother,' Daphne wound up, with more truth than tact. 'Anyway, if you could just keep an eye on him for the next two or three hours, I'll pick him up on my way home. And tell him he's been an extremely naughty little boy and Mummy's really cross with him.' She rang off without saying goodbye or, indeed, thank you.

'And *you* don't know what it's like having someone else's child dumped on you when you have an article to finish,' Morgan retorted, but only to herself. She went back into the kitchen and said, 'Your mum says you're to stay and have supper with Lin and me. Oh, and I'm to tell you she's not best pleased with you.'

Ollie managed a shaky grin. 'I bet that's not how she put it.'

'Not exactly, but that was the gist.' She sat down at the table and listened to Inspector Burdock summing up his interview with Ollie.

'All right, lad, you're sure the cat was the property of a Dr Elspeth Blair-Guthrie, at present in South America but returning shortly. You last saw it alive on Friday morning. You reported it as stolen at Oxbourne police station on Saturday as a consequence of suspecting a possible intruder in Dr Blair-Guthrie's flat, but you found nothing else missing or disarranged apart from a cushion. Is that correct?'

'Yes, it is. And he was a he-cat. His name was Alka-Seltzer.'

'Alka-Seltzer, was it, sonny? I'll just make a note of that.'

'It's a pity that other policeman didn't bother to write down what I told him,' said Oliver severely.

After Inspector Burdock had gone, Morgan and Oliver eyed each other warily, wondering how they were going to get through the hour or so of each other's company until Lin got back from London. Morgan thought that Ollie was still looking tense and fragile. She reminded herself that at his age the loss of an animal could be worse than losing a person. She herself was still wincing away from the thought of how the police were going to break this latest development to Libby and James. Daphne was right. She didn't know what it was to be a mother, and at this moment she was more than glad.

She said tentatively to Ollie, 'Do you want to talk about it?'

The child shrugged. 'Not really,' he said listlessly. There was a long pause and then he burst out passionately, 'I mean, it was all right him dying in the forest. He wasn't a tame cat, he was a hunter. But making fun of him like that, taking away his ...' He couldn't find the word he wanted.

'His dignity,' suggested Morgan.

'More than that. He should have died like a mighty hunter and instead they just made him look silly.' Angry tears filled his eyes and were fiercely blinked back. 'He wasn't just an ordinary cat. He was special.'

'Like Blake's tyger,' said Morgan.

'What's that?'

'I'll find it for you.'

Oliver studied the poem severely, testing it against his sense of Alka-Seltzer's violated honour. 'I like the bit about symmetry,' he said grudgingly, 'but whoever drew that tiger couldn't paint for toffee.'

'Why not do a better one, then? Elspeth's going to be pretty upset when she hears about Alka-Seltzer. It would help her a lot to have a really good picture of him.' Generously, she unhooked her apron from the back of the kitchen door. 'Here, you'll need this.'

When Lin arrived home, she found Morgan cooking with a dishcloth pinned round her waist and Oliver furiously at work in the studio. Once again he had painted a dark and tangled forest but this time a coffin-like black box decorated with a string of multi-coloured blobs lay at the bottom of the picture-space while above it a great orange and black striped animal glowered magnificently through the trees, his bared fangs and blazing eyes displaying a fearful symmetry.

CHAPTER NINE

Libby came back from identifying Ben's cot blanket and Babygro shaking uncontrollably and with her teeth chattering. WPC Davis ushered her into the house, where Octavia took one look at her and decided that strong measures were called for.

'You've got to get away from here, Libby. Go to London for a few days. It'll do James good to be able to feel he's looking after you. I'll get Dick to drive you there in the morning – you're in no state to be behind a steering-wheel.'

'I have to stay here,' said Libby wearily. 'Suppose the kidnapper tries to get in touch when the house is empty.'

'Don't talk nonsense, Libby. I shall be manning the fort.'

'You can't leave Dick to cope with Melanie and the boys on his own,' Libby protested. 'Doesn't he have a book to finish?'

'Melanie is no trouble – we hardly know we've got her. And the boys can stay with Granny Castlemain until school starts. She'll love that and it'll do them no harm. Good training for putting up with crashing bores in later life.'

'Poor kids,' said Libby doubtfully.

'Poor kids, nothing. Keep them out of mischief. We don't need any more young detectives round here.'

In fact the message which arrived some days later was a letter addressed to James Gilbert at his London hospital and enclosed in a brown business envelope franked with an indecipherable postmark. By the time it was delivered, there had already been a number of other developments in the case.

Inspector Burdock had never met Octavia Castlemain, but he would have heartily approved of her views on young detectives. The ongoing saga of Ben's kidnapping was by now selling newspapers all over Britain. After some hesitation, Inspector Burdock had released the story of the finding of Alka-Seltzer to the press, though without going into details about the identity of the small boy who had made the discovery.

'We can't play it close to our chests when that wretched kid knows all about it. Seems he's some kind of media star, or so my wife tells me. As if we didn't have troubles enough on this case. Anyway, it's such a kinky angle, it may just jerk someone's memory about something.'

In this, Inspector Burdock did Oliver an injustice. He had spoken of Alka-Seltzer's death to no one. It was an enterprising journalist from the *Daily Mail* who ferreted round the village, discovered that a child had gone temporarily missing on the day the pram was found and decided to follow up his hunch that there might be a connection. He looked up the Cresswell address, located the house and rang the bell. It was simply his good luck that it was Oliver who opened the door.

'Hi,' he said, grinning matily at the unprepossessing child on the doorstep. 'You must be Oliver, right? The one who found the cat.'

Oliver was startled into asking, 'How did you know that?'

'We have our methods, Carruthers. Like to tell me all about it?'

'No thanks,' said Oliver and shut the door, but he had already given away the only fact that mattered.

It was not until he reported his discovery and was asked, 'You mean, *the* Oliver Cresswell?' that the *Mail* man realised the size of his scoop. The perfect front page story and no need to skulk around trying to snatch a photograph either.

Daphne had read about the finding of Alka-Seltzer in the *Telegraph* – 'New Twist in Baby Kidnap Case' – but she naturally never saw a copy of the *Mail*, and the rest of the village, taking in the story with a mixture of shock and enjoyment over breakfast, didn't think to enlighten her. It was not until she opened the front door on a knot of reporters and press photographers asking for Oliver that she realised he had any connection with the affair. A clip of her flustered attempts to sweep them off her doorstep made the ITV News.

Oliver was not allowed to read the resulting coverage; Inspector Burdock was not so lucky. Under banner headlines – 'BOY TEC IN KIDNAP HORROR', 'EGGHEAD KID'S BABY CASE CLUE' – and alongside earnest pictures of Oliver clutching his A level certificates, were articles inquiring nastily why the only progress in the case so far had been made by a ten-year-old boy and when were the police going to act.

Oliver found himself being ferried everywhere by car for several days. To Daphne's frantic questioning – 'Why didn't you *tell* Mummy, Ollie darling?' – he simply replied that he hadn't thought the police wanted people to know. He had become quieter and more detached than ever. A slow-burning anger was smouldering inside him. Someone had killed Alka-Seltzer and dishonoured his corpse; Oliver didn't know how he was going to punish that person, but he would do it somehow.

Inspector Burdock was equally determined and equally baffled as to how to proceed. Extensive police inquiries throughout the area, and the following up of all responses to Mrs Gilbert's television appearance, had so far yielded nothing, leaving him to puzzle yet again over the only evidence he had. The cat had a broken neck, otherwise there was not a mark on it. Both the pram and the plastic-covered mattress inside it had been wiped clean, presumably before being dumped in the wood, but there were a number of blurred prints on the chromium-plated handle, prints which seemed too small to have been made by an adult hand. A painstaking search had produced no evidence as to how the pram had reached the clearing, which was not really surprising given its light weight and the fact that the carry-cot body and the wheeled base could each be carried in one hand. However, it was obvious from the crushed vegetation that once actually in the clearing it had been wheeled to and fro, presumably by the owner of the prints.

'And if it was a kid, then it wasn't young Oliver. He swears he never laid a finger on that pram.'

'Do you reckon it could have been a kid that took the baby, sir?' asked Sergeant Crewe.

'Shouldn't think so. Whoever took Ben must have wiped the pram, and that can't have been the person who left those prints.' Inspector Burdock sighed heavily. 'The real question is, who put the cat in the pram? If it was just some kid playing about then it gets us no further. But if young Oliver is right and someone stole the cat, then maybe that same someone took Ben. *And* killed the cat and dressed it up in Ben's clothes. And in that case we've got a real lunatic out there, and he's still got little Ben Gilbert.'

There was a sombre silence and then Sergeant Crewe said quietly, 'Let's just hope he's still got little Ben Gilbert.'

CHAPTER TEN

Richard Castlemain seldom thought about his own emotions, so he didn't actually tell himself what a relief it was to have the house to himself for a change. Fond though he supposed himself to be of his wife and sons, he usually expended a good deal of negative energy tuning out the sound of Octavia's voice, Jack's electric guitar, and Sebastian's feet on the stairs. The unaccustomed silence was conducive to his work and he seldom emerged from his study.

Melanie, as Octavia had told Libby, was a barely noticeable presence. She hardly spoke, hardly ate, crept around like a frightened mouse and spent most of her time in her room. She tried to make herself useful by occasionally filling the dishwasher or the washing machine, but Richard wasn't interested in housework, only in peace and quiet. He himself did such minimal cooking as was needed, heating up food from the freezer according to the rota which Octavia had left him.

He was not an unfeeling man, simply a preoccupied and absent-minded one, and if he had realised the depth of

Melanie's loneliness and misery he would have tried to do something about it, even if it was only alerting Octavia to the problem. As it was, he peacefully ignored her, and Melanie was timidly grateful. All she wanted was to be left alone. She spent as much time as possible lying on her bed in a shallow half-sleep which left her permanently headachy and lethargic but eliminated the need to think. To think was to be reminded of Ben and that was more than she could bear.

On Thursdays, Mrs Boswell always came to do the cleaning. She knew better than to venture into the professor's study but she turned Melanie out of the spare room while she hoovered and changed the bed. Melanie wandered restlessly into the kitchen, where Mrs Boswell's copy of the *Mail* was lying on the table, ready to add spice to her mid-morning cuppa. The headline jumped out at Melanie: BCY TEC IN KIDNAP HORROR. Kidnap could only mean Ben. Queasily, unable to stop herself, she read the story.

It was just as well, as Octavia herself was to remark more than once during the days that followed, that that afternoon she left one of the Woodcraft mums on duty in the Gilberts' house while she herself came home to stock up the fridge freezer. It was she who discovered Melanie lying unconscious in her room, she who phoned for the ambulance, she who discovered the empty sleeping pill bottle where it had rolled under the bed, she who alerted the university authorities to the

75

fact that Melanie Wilson was in Oxbourne Infirmary after an unsuccessful suicide attempt.

Morgan was not best pleased to be phoned up by Rupert Allison with the news that Melanie was in hospital.

'You're her personal tutor, Rupert, for heaven's sake. She's your responsibility.'

'Well, yes, but under the circumstances I thought a woman's touch and all that. Shoulder to cry on. You know the kind of thing. And anyway, Valerie's staying with her mother and Joshua's teething and I've got to get this article finished by the start of term. So if you'd be a sweetie.'

'Women aren't allowed to drop everything just because their babies are teething, Rupert, so why should you?' said Morgan, enraged.

'Well I can't take him with me to the hospital, can I? I mean, babies are a bit of a sore subject under the circs. If the Gilbert child hadn't been kidnapped, Melanie wouldn't even be there.'

'All right, all right. I'll do it. But just remember that you owe me. You're not the only one with an article to finish.'

Cursing, Morgan phoned the hospital and was relieved to be told that it would be a few days before Melanie would be in any state for visitors. She knew perfectly well that it was not simply Joshua's teething which had made Rupert so unwilling to get involved but normal selfish male terror at the possibility of being caught in the octopus clutches of someone else's despair, augmented in this case by the unexamined and irrational belief that to go anywhere near the girl who had mislaid the Gilberts' baby was to invite harm by association to his own child. Morgan resented being landed with the feelings of guilt that Rupert had so successfully evaded almost as much as she dreaded the forthcoming interview with Melanie. She hated hospital visiting at the best of times and in this case she could think of no possible consolation to offer. The memory of the dead cat wrapped in Ben Gilbert's cot blanket was still too nastily vivid.

The mingled flavours of duty, reluctance and guilt brought another obligation to mind. She had not seen anything of Rosalind Gilbert since the morning after Ben went missing and she was uneasily aware that she ought to have done. Rosalind might well be nearly as distressed as Melanie. After all, the kidnapped child was her nephew. Cursing again at her own overactive conscience, Morgan picked up her phone. Rosalind sounded both edgy and wary, very much as Rupert had done, as if she too felt that any contact with the outside world might somehow endanger Persephone Jane. However, she agreed that it was some time since they had discussed her thesis and suggested, in the manner of someone conferring a favour, that Morgan could drop round at tea-time.

Since Rosalind, like her sister-in-law, lived near the university campus, Morgan decided to call in at the department first to check her mail and do a few routine tasks. Term would be starting soon and she had reading lists to complete. As she emerged from the Arts Building, still leafing idly through a pile of the useless paper which invariably silts up academic pigeonholes, she ran into Collington who greeted her with lugubrious satisfaction.

'Afternoon, Dr Byrd, miss. Shocking thing about young Melanie Wilson.'

'Terrible, yes,' said Morgan crisply, not sorry to be able to deprive him for once of the pleasure of breaking bad news.

'Mind, it's not as if I was really surprised when I heard,' confided Collington, unabashed. 'Fact, I reckon that with half an eye I could've seen it coming. All that living on half a lettuce leaf and calling it kindness to animals. Not to mention that trouble last term.'

Rather against the grain, Morgan asked, 'What trouble last term?'

'Why, her young man being given the heave-ho like that. Must have upset her, stands to reason.'

Mentally acknowledging that Collington had won this round hands down, Morgan said, 'I didn't know she had a young man. She always seems to be on her own.'

'She used to go around with that lad in Philosophy. What was he called now? I'll be forgetting my own name next. Organised that demo outside the Mouse House. Shocking lot of mess they made, too.'

'Lawrence Craik? The one who was sent down?'

'That's right, miss. He used to see quite a bit of young Melanie. And she's the kind to take it hard, losing her boyfriend. Well, there. I dare say you can remember what it feels like yourself, miss.'

Morgan dumped her mail on the back seat of the car and drove the short distance to the Gilberts' house feeling that this was definitely not her day. The first thing she saw when Rosalind opened the door to her was Persephone's pram standing in the hall. The involuntary flashback to the incident in Hangman's Wood made her feel slightly nauseous for a moment. Persephone herself, dressed in pink frills, was tightly clutched in her mother's arms. Scrutinising the soft blob of a face under the transparently frail wisps of hair, Morgan wondered how on earth mothers ever told their babies apart. She managed a few appropriate noises, to which the infant responded by dribbling slightly down its lacy bib.

Rosalind too, she discovered wryly over the Earl Grey tea and digestive biscuits, was suffering from superstitious feelings of guilt and fear. Instead of discussing the latest chapter of her thesis, she began compulsively telling Morgan how relieved she was that Libby had gone to London and how bad she felt about not having seen her since Ben was taken.

'I know it must seem heartless, but I just don't feel I can leave Zeffie with a sitter, not after what's happened. And how could I take her round to Libby's? It would be too unkind. I mean, she's just the same size as poor little Ben, what with being so premature, though she was born over two months earlier. And it's so dreadful to lose a child. I know I should be able to share that with Libby, but I can't, I really can't. I wouldn't know what to say to her.'

As she spoke, she kept twisting her fingers together in a miserable way, looking positively haunted by her own failure to come to terms with Libby's loss. Morgan, all too clearly reminded of her own feelings about visiting Melanie, made tactfully non-committal noises. Presently Persephone began wailing fretfully and Morgan found herself a reluctant witness to the distasteful business of nappy-changing. It occurred to her that one of the most dreadful things about being a baby was the complete lack of privacy it involved. Still, at least the ritual application of zinc ointment and dusting powder seemed to cheer Rosalind up a bit. When Persephone was safely bundled up in fresh padding, Morgan firmly steered the conversation round to multiple chronologies in *Sir Charles Grandison*.

Melanie, meanwhile, lay in a shadowy state of half-being while the sedatives and the nightmare fought for possession of her breaking mind. She barely noticed the ministrations of the nurses or the visits from the psychiatrist. She ignored the tepid plates of tasteless food just as she ignored the too cheerful words of these useless helpers. When night came, she sank into a pit of blackness in which the nightmare lurked and pounced, so that she woke sweating. Dawn brought back the nurses with their drugs trolley and their unwanted cups of tea. She lay through that day and the days that followed, listless, unresponsive, silent, staring at nothingness with fixed, unseeing eyes.

CHAPTER ELEVEN

Monday brought the start of the school term, and for once Oliver was glad. The atmosphere at home had been sultry and unstable ever since the media and his mother had found out about Alka-Seltzer's death. At break he found himself unexpectedly popular until the other kids realised he wasn't going to tell them anything. He also found he had a new nickname.

'Come on, Sherlock, tell us what you told the cops.'

'It's confidential information,' said Oliver grandly.

'It was all in the papers.'

'They don't know anything. They just make things up.'

When they went in from the playground, they were surprised to find themselves being shepherded into the hall. Mrs Ross, the head teacher, looking unusually solemn, was sitting on the platform next to a lady in police uniform. A stir of excitement mixed with guilt, irrational but instinctive, passed through the rows of children as they settled into their places. Only Oliver was unmoved. He was pretty sure he knew what was coming.

Mrs Ross said, 'Now children, this is Sergeant Blossom.' No one dared to nudge or giggle at the name. 'She's come to ask us a few questions. You probably all know that a baby has been stolen and the police are trying to find him. Well, Sergeant Blossom thinks that one of you may know something which will help, so please listen carefully. And remember, there's nothing to worry about. No one is going to be cross with you.'

Sergeant Blossom had a cheery, down-to-earth manner. She explained about little Ben's pram being found in Hangman's Wood with a cat dressed up as a baby inside it.

'Now, we think that someone may have been playing in that part of the wood, so we're going round all the local schools to ask if anyone knows anything about that pram. It's possible someone may have been playing at dollies with it. Now, like your teacher said, we're not cross with you. You haven't done anything naughty. But if you saw that pram, you may be able to help us get little Ben Gilbert back to his Mum and Dad.

'OK, in a moment I'm going to ask anyone who saw the pram to hold up their hand. But if you don't want to do that, you can tell your class teacher about it quietly when you go back to your classroom. So, does anyone have anything to tell me?'

A rustle ran through the children but no hand was raised. Oliver was sitting behind Cathy and Stephanie, that inseparable pair of friends. He expected them to nudge each other in the silly way they usually did, but instead they stiffened and sat very still. Mindful that he was now Sherlock Cresswell, he continued to watch them as everyone filed out of the hall and saw Stephanie edge forward in the line until she was level with Danny Brown, a rather slow-witted boy, small for his age and not very popular though not as friendless as Oliver himself. She kicked him slyly on the ankle and then, when he turned a startled face in her direction, gave him a warning frown and shook her head.

Oliver waited until the lunchtime break and then cornered Danny quietly and led him behind the cycle shed. It wasn't difficult; Danny was a docile boy who mostly did what he was told.

'All right,' said Oliver fiercely, trying to sound like a proper detective. 'You know something about that pram, don't you?'

'How did you know?' asked Danny, just as Oliver himself had done to the reporter.

'I have my methods,' said Oliver. 'You know something, and so do Stephanie and Cathy, and either you tell me or I'm going to tell Mrs Ross.'

'Then you'd be a rotten telltale,' said Danny, vainly trying an appeal to the solidarity of children against the adult world, 'and no one would ever speak to you again.'

'I'd be helping the police with their inquiries,' said Oliver, unmoved.

Danny looked at Oliver in a hunted way. 'It wasn't my fault,' he said desperately. 'They made me do it. They'll kill me if we get found out.'

'Made you do what?' asked Oliver inexorably.

Danny went red and his whole body wriggled with embarrassment. He muttered reluctantly, 'We were playing Black Bag.'

'What's that?'

'*You* know,' said Danny hopefully.

Oliver shook his head.

In a rush, as if he suddenly needed to get the secret out, Danny whispered, 'One of them's a lady having a baby and she lies down and takes her knickers off. And the boy is the doctor and he has to look and see if the baby's coming. And the other one is the nurse and she puts the baby in the cot. They take turns. They make all the boys play it. They mostly use a teddy for the baby, but this time it was a cat.'

Even Oliver, who had no interest in girls, could see that this had to be concealed from the grown-ups. Some things are taboo, and this was one of them.

He thought for a moment and then said, 'I know! You'll have to send an anonymous letter. I'll do it for you, if you like.'

'What's that?'

'A letter saying that Cathy and Stephanie know about the pram, but without your name on it.'

'Mrs Ross would recognise the writing.'

'I can do it on my laptop.'

'But if Cathy and Stephanie get in trouble, they'll tell on me.'

'No they won't,' said Oliver with adult cynicism. 'They'll just look all sweet and innocent and say they were playing at dollies like that police lady said. No one will guess a thing.'

The letter was easy enough to write; the only difficulty was getting hold of a stamp. Oliver could neither ask for one without explaining why he needed it nor buy one in the village shop without arousing suspicion. It took a couple of days before he managed to sneak one out of Daphne's handbag, by which time Danny had happily forgotten about the whole thing.

The letter which eventually arrived on Inspector Burdock's desk was short and to the point.

To Who It May Concern

I have reason to believe that Stephanie Smith and Cathy Mitchell in class 5 Freshley Village School have information which may assist your inquiries.

Ask them who put Alkerselser in the pram.

Yours respectfully,

An Ancnymous Correspondent

Oliver had taken pains over its composition and his spell-check had only let him down over a single word.

CHAPTER TWELVE

After the frenzied pace of San Lorenzo, London looked clean and slow and peaceful, a city with green spaces where it was still possible to walk alone in the spring sunshine. Even the conspicuous signs of poverty and social decay – the empty shops, the homeless people huddled in doorways – failed to shake Elspeth's buoyant mood. It was the sight of the car that did that. She spotted it again as she got out of the taxi at Kensington Gardens. She was almost sure now that she had seen it at the airport and certain that it had been outside the hotel.

I'm probably just a paranoid old woman, she told herself firmly. Anyway, they won't get much useful information from the sight of an elderly aunt going for a quiet stroll with her nephew. Leaning heavily on her stick, she made her way towards the bench where she had arranged to meet Torquil. A wizened little man with protruding ears, wearing a cloth cap and a muffler despite the warmth of the day, was already sitting at one end of it reading the *Daily Mail* and sharing the crumbs from a sandwich wrapper with a couple of pigeons. He looked like the embodiment of a vanished London, as if he had spent every afternoon there since the Blitz.

Elspeth sank down onto the other end of the bench. She was a little early and Torquil, a notoriously busy man, would almost certainly be late. For a while she watched the passing strollers, half-seriously trying to pick out the men in the blue BMW from among them, but they all looked like harmless tourists. Presently her attention was drawn to the newspaper which her companion was holding. Elspeth, who still took the *Scotsman* every day in addition to the *Guardian*, had little interest in the tabloid press but she had the common academic vice of being unable to prevent herself from reading any kind of print that fell under her eye. Besides, she had not seen an English paper for several weeks. In San Lorenzo she had had to make do with an occasional copy of the *Washington Post*.

The lead story, which seemed to concern a piece of trivial and uncorroborated gossip about a minor member of the royal family, was illustrated by a picture of a girl getting into a sports car. She had obviously just turned her head in response to a shout from the photographer, and her face wore the feral but defenceless look of a vixen caught in headlights. There was second story further down the page. Elspeth craned forward a little to make it out, telling herself for the hundredth time that she really must go and have her eyes tested again. Like the letters on the optician's chart, she managed to spell out the headline.

In her precise Scottish voice she said, 'Excuse me, would you mind if I borrowed your paper for a moment?'

'You tyke it, lidy,' said the little man, rising to his feet and folding up his sandwich wrapper. 'You tyke it. It's a bit aht a date but the noos is always the same reely, ain't it. There you go, you little bleeders, that's yer lot,' he added amiably to the disappointed pigeons.

When Torquil arrived, Elspeth was still peering intently at the article and the photograph that illustrated it, an eight-year-old Oliver disdainfully holding up his A level certificates for the camera.

'Hallo, Aunt Eppie. I didn't know you read the *Mail*.'

'I don't, but perhaps I should. It appears that there has been a kidnapping. Someone has taken James Gilbert's baby and apparently left a dead cat in its place. But that wasn't what I wanted to talk to you about, Torquil. Could we perhaps find a more secluded spot?'

'Come back and have some coffee at the House and then we can have a private chat in my office. There isn't anything wrong is there, Aunt Eppie?'

'Wrong, dear? No, I don't think so, but I have been wanting to rearrange my affairs and I should welcome your advice.'

The shocks and media assaults of the last twelve days had made Sister Maxwell fiercely and tenaciously protective both of James Gilbert's privacy and of the sanctity of her ward. Not that this gaunt white-haired woman in her baggy tweed suit looked anything like a reporter, but Sister had reached the point of taking no chances.

'I'm sorry,' she said firmly and with no regret at all. 'Only close relatives are allowed to visit our babies and Mr Gilbert sees no one without an appointment.'

'He will see me,' replied Elspeth equally firmly. Her voice, pitched at its most Edinburgh genteel, calmly pulled rank. 'I have a message for him from his brother. Tell him that Dr Blair-Guthrie wishes to see him,' she added, unfairly notching up medical kudos for a DPhil in anthropology. 'And in the meantime I should like to speak to Mrs Potter if she is here. You have her son Isaac among your patients.'

Sister Maxwell hesitated, then softened. 'Oh, you mean little Ishmael Potter. Yes, his mother is here, poor thing. She hardly leaves him. He's doing fine as far as we know but she can't seem to stop worrying about him. I'll let her know you're here. She could do with a bit of company and that's a fact.'

Elspeth was shocked by her first sight of Naomi Potter. She seemed to have aged ten years in as many weeks and she had a troubled, uncertain air, quite unlike her earlier stern resolve.

Instead of the long print dress and black headscarf which marked women out as belonging to the Sealed Brethren, she was wearing a neat but shabby skirt and blouse which looked as if they had come from a charity jumble sale. Her hair was still pinned up in the sober braids she had worn since her marriage but she had taken off her wedding ring.

The child for whose sake she had derailed her life was lying in a Perspex crib surrounded by gleaming machines and with so many tubes and wires attached to his frail little body that it was hard to think of him as completely human. Elspeth bent over him, trying to think of the right thing to say.

'Sister tells me he's doing well.'

Naomi's voice was low and expressionless as if she had long ago exhausted all possible emotion. 'So they say. It may be so. Do you think I've done right by him, Elspeth Blair-Guthrie?' The question was barely a question, more a weary statement of fact.

'You did what you had to, Naomi.'

'Through me he's got no father and no name.'

'Then Enoch ...?'

'Enoch is not to be blamed. I told him the child was none of his. He'd never've consented to let me go, else. I've thrown away the child's name and my own name. They cast me out and my son with me. I can never return to the Brethren.'

'But your son is alive, Naomi.'

'Instead of with God. That's two fathers I've taken him from, if you think rightly.'

'I can't believe that God would blame you for that, Naomi.'

Naomi stared hard at her, the listless expression giving way to bitterness. 'How do you know what God would blame me for, Elspeth Blair-Guthrie? How do you know what laws I've broken?'

'I don't, of course,' said Elspeth dryly, tackling the question with academic fair-mindedness. 'But unless God is just, his laws can't be real laws, and I can't reasonably believe in a just God who would condemn a mother for saving her child's life. Nor can I believe in a God so powerless that Isaac could survive without his intending it to happen. Anyway,' she added, partly to salve her own conscience as a convinced and usually truthful atheist, 'when I was sent to Sunday school as a child, they taught us that the Sabbath was made for man, not man for the Sabbath. We are not meant to make an idol of the law if harm will result from it.'

This flinging down of a scriptural gauntlet stiffened Naomi into resistance. 'It says in the Book that we are not to do evil that good may come. And that the sins of the fathers shall be visited on the children, yea unto the fourth generation.'

'It's not God who punishes children for their fathers' sins,' said Elspeth robustly, 'it's other human beings. You haven't done evil, Naomi. You have done what you had to do.'

93

Naomi's defiance faded into apology. 'It's not that I'm ungrateful for the help you gave us, Elspeth Blair-Guthrie. I know you advised me according to your lights. But I couldn't have done what you said. I couldn't have let the lawyers wrangle over my child's life or death and have it in the papers for all to read. Besides, the Brethren would have cast him out in any case once the surgeon had touched him. How could I have let him go into the wilderness alone. At least this way our marriage is cancelled out and Enoch can take another wife and maybe get another son. But I can have no other son. Only Ishmael. Only Ishmael.'

'Don't call him that, Naomi. His name is Isaac.'

'Ishmael is the name his father gave him when he turned us from his house. Should a child not be known by the name his father gave him?'

Elspeth sighed. This particular rhetorical question was one it seemed better not to answer. She said, 'I'm sorry, Naomi. It's been hard for you, all this.'

'The hardest is to be cast out from the Brethren to live among strangers and sinners all my life. You cannot know how hard that is, Elspeth Blair-Guthrie.'

The anthropologist in Elspeth responded with the irrepressible thought that it would indeed be interesting to know what it was like. It was rare for the Sealed Brethren to cast out any of their members. Mentally she pulled herself back to attention. Searching for some scrap of comfort to offer, she again recalled those childhood hours of dreamy boredom in the kirk at Blair Easton, listening to the minister's highland singsong as he instructed the village children in his own version of Christianity.

She said, 'There are maybe worse people to know. Didn't Jesus spend a lot of his time with sinners.'

Slow tears began to run down Naomi's cheeks. 'Like me,' she whispered. She began to gasp and shudder into sobs, hiding her face in her hands.

Sister Maxwell appeared in the doorway and came briskly over to pat Naomi on the shoulder. 'That's right, dear,' she said, with routine kindness, 'You have a good cry. I'll send one of my nurses in with a cup of tea.' And then, as Naomi shook her head inarticulately at the mention of this forbidden beverage, 'Don't be silly, dear, a nice cup of tea will do you a power of good. Call it doctor's orders. Oh, and Mr Gilbert will see you now, Dr Blaine-Duffy,' she added, steering Elspeth firmly out of the ward.

Elspeth followed the sharply clacking heels down the cream-painted hospital corridor feeling troubled not only by Naomi Potter's distress and the probably even more painful interview with James Gilbert still to come, but also by her own involvement in other people's affairs. She was an anthropologist. It was her job to study self-contained societies like the Kainu and the Sealed Brethren, not to interfere in them. It was true that both Aapuulo and Naomi had asked for her help, it was true that both the survival of the tribe and the life of a child were at stake, but how could she know whether she had done the right thing in either case. Isaac Potter might still die, and then Naomi would have lost everything. Might it not have been better for her at least to have a husband to grieve with. And the legal arrangements that she had drawn up with Torquil's expert help, would they really be sufficient to safeguard the tribe, and for that matter to safeguard young Oliver, whose destiny she had presumed to meddle with in such a cavalier fashion? 'The Deil finds wark for toom haunds,' her nanny used to tell her. She would just have to hope she had the Deil's luck as well.

In a way, James's rigid self-control was even harder to deal with than Naomi's drained despair. He sat behind his desk, his face as professionally impassive as if she had come to consult him about her arthritis, and Elspeth felt the words dry up in her mouth.

'I take it you've heard about Ben.'

'I didn't find out until yesterday. James, I'm so sorry. Is Libby ...?'

'Bearing up.'

'Have they any idea ...?'

'Not as yet. But this came in today's post. I suppose you'd better not touch it.'

He picked up a sheet of paper gingerly by one corner and laid it on the desk in front of her. The message had been produced on a cheap computer printer and consisted of a single sentence:

WE'VE DONE NOTHING TO YOUR BABY THAT YOU AND YOUR BROTHER HAVEN'T DONE TO HELPLESS MONKEYS.

Elspeth felt her stomach turn over. She said, 'Do the police ...?'

'I've just rung them. It may well be a hoax, of course.'

'Yes, I expect so. Some inadequate person looking for a bit of attention.' Elspeth fumbled in her handbag. 'James dear, I know this is a bad time, but Andrew asked me to give you this.'

Mechanically, James took the envelope, ripped it open, glanced through Andrew's letter and put it down on the desk.

He said, 'Andrew never could face up to things. Has he told Rosalind?'

'Before he left for San Lorenzo.'

'Well, at least he'll earn more with Gifford Pharmaceuticals than he would ever have done at Oxbourne University. Who is the girl? Have you met her?'

'No, I haven't, dear. I gather she's someone he met in Chicago the last time he went over. I don't think that he and Rosalind have been getting on for some time.'

'Not since the twins were born. Rosalind took that very hard, you know. Well, I suppose he won't be seeing much of Persephone Jane from now on.' His face twisted and he picked up Andrew's letter and crumpled it into a ball. 'It's his life, the bloody stupid bastard. Let him bloody well get on with it.'

CHAPTER THIRTEEN

Inspector Burdock was inclined to share James Gilbert's scepticism about the threatening letter.

'If this is some joker messing us about, I'll have his balls for it,' he told Sergeant Crewe irritably. His lack of progress on the case was beginning to affect his nerves.

'Supposing it's genuine, sir, what does it tell us?'

'Bleeder posted it in some town with seven or eight letters to its name. Christ, you'd think the Royal Mail could at least have given us a legible postmark. He's probably fairly well-educated – knows how to spell the plural of monkey, at any rate, and puts the apostrophes in the right places. No ransom demand, but he may just be trying to soften the Gilberts up at this stage. He says "we" and not "I", so there's a possibility that he belongs to some sort of animal rights group – I suppose we can follow that one up, at least. But he may just be a lone nutter trying to sound more menacing. Nasty veiled threat, but ambiguously worded. Doesn't say what he *has* done, only what he hasn't. Fact, he doesn't actually say he's ever set eyes on little Ben Gilbert. Twenty to one, it's a hoax.'

'What *did* the Gilbert brothers do to those monkeys, sir?'

'Pumped them full of some experimental drug, apparently, and then did a tricky operation on their livers. Our joker can't have done any of that. But it seems that all lab animals have to be put down once the experiment is over. Official regulations.' He met Sergeant Crewe's eyes and looked away again. There was a moment of rather nasty silence.

'Haven't forensics come up with anything, sir?' asked Sergeant Crewe, breaking the tension.

'No joy there either. No fingerprints on the letter itself except James Gilbert's. Several on the envelope, of course, but that's no good to us. They reckon the paper and envelope were bought in WH Smiths. One of those in just about every town in the country. Oh, and they think he did it on a MacBook. Fat lot of use.'

'We've just bought our Eleanor one of those for her homework. Amazing gadgets, really, when you think. But you're right, sir. It's not much help with our joker here. Half the students in the country probably have one, for a start.'

'Including our other anonymous correspondent, young Oliver Cresswell. In one of those old-fashioned detective stories, I suppose that would be the vital clue. An upper-case "E" out of alignment and Bob's your uncle.'

Sergeant Crewe grinned. 'I don't really see you as Miss Marple, sir.'

'Hang on a minute, though. You said students. If our joker is an animal lover, that might fit. Didn't they have a bit of trouble up at the university last term? Doesn't fit so well with bumping off the cat, though, always supposing it was the kidnapper who did that.'

'I'll just see if Cherry's back.' Inspector Burdock raised a questioning eyebrow. 'Sergeant Blossom, sir. Everyone calls her Cherry. She was interviewing those Freshley kids this morning.'

Mary Blossom had found Cathy and Stephanie a fairly tiresome pair, giggling nervously and exchanging knowing glances, but they had had a quite coherent story to tell. They had found the pram in the clearing, with the Babygro and blanket neatly folded inside. They had passed the cat on their way into the wood, near to the roadside, and had gone back to fetch it in order to play at mothers and babies. They hadn't owned up before because their parents didn't allow them to go into Hangman's Wood on their own.

'Just another red herring, then. I sometimes think this bleeding case consists of nothing else,' said Inspector Burdock wearily. 'Well, I suppose it simplifies things. I was beginning to wonder if we shouldn't have young Oliver in again, ask him if he could remember anything else about that intruder he thought he heard. There are too many bleeding kids in this case, if you ask ...'

He was interrupted in mid-grumble by the phone ringing.

'Oxbourne and District CID. Burdock speaking. Yes. Yes, that is correct. Yes. She said *what*? All right, we're on our way.'

When Morgan arrived at the hospital, she discovered that Rupert's defection had landed her with appearing to be Melanie's personal tutor. She was taken aside and interviewed by a brusque psychiatrist who clearly thought it very remiss of her not to have spotted earlier warning signs of suicidal tendencies. Like Rupert, he seemed to imagine that the job of a female university tutor was to be a professional shoulder to cry on. Stifling the urge to protest that she had never so much as taught the kid, Morgan asked how she was doing.

'It's not easy to make a firm diagnosis at this stage. She's obviously very shocked and disturbed by this kidnap affair. In fact, she hasn't spoken at all since we've had her here. However, she might open up a bit more to someone she connects with a structured part of her life. Don't mention the Baby Gilbert business, though. We think that reading a newspaper article about the case may have been what sparked off this little episode, so we have thought it best to shield her from more recent developments. Just talk about everyday things in a normal way. She's in Room 6, down the corridor on the left.'

Morgan set off down the corridor, wondering how you held a normal conversation about everyday things with someone too disturbed to speak and wincing at the thought of the most recent developments in the kidnap case. The police had decided to release the anonymous letter, on the grounds that keeping up the pressure of publicity offered the best hope of finding Ben, if indeed he was still alive. Libby had made a second television appeal, with James sitting rigid and silent by her side. It had been decided not to let him speak, both because, unlike Libby, he was plainly not going to hit the right emotional note and because it had seemed wiser to take a more oblique approach to the issue of the Gilbert brothers' animal experiments.

Libby had been white-faced and tense, but she had managed to deliver her lines with a moving clarity and poise.

'Ben is just a baby, an innocent baby who never harmed anyone in his life. He doesn't deserve to be taken away from his home and his parents. Please, if anyone watching knows where he is, or has noticed anything unusual, get in touch with the police. If you've ever had a child, you will know just how precious Ben is to us. Please help us to get him back. We miss him so terribly.'

Libby had scripted the message with Octavia's help and had rehearsed until she could say it without a tremor, except for the last sentence. The break which came into her voice at that point was heart-rending in its suggestion of courage and pain. Libby herself was amazed at the facility with which she was able to project a synthetic version of her own suffering, the ease with which she could let her eyes fill with telegenic tears. If this travesty was what it took to get Ben back, there was no emotion, however private, that she would not willingly put on public display. She was aware that her performance was yet another wedge in the crevasse that was opening between herself and James, but she no longer cared. The slender hope of recovering Ben had become the only thing that mattered. To allow herself to think about what James was feeling would have meant confronting his growing certainty that Ben was dead.

Morgan, knocking gently on the door of Room 6, thought that it was indeed just as well that Melanie, burdened with guilt as she must doubtless be, had not had to watch Libby's appeal. Receiving no reply, she knocked a second time, then opened the door. The room was bare but bright in a heartless, institutional way. Melanie, with a hospital nametag fastened round her wrist, was sitting fully dressed on the side of the bed, staring in front of her with a haggard zombie face. She neither spoke nor moved when Morgan came in. Her hunched back fended off the intrusion, as if she was still alone in the room. Morgan wished passionately that Lin was here sharing this gruesome experience with her. One of the advantages of being deaf, she reflected ruefully, was getting out of situations like this.

Tentatively she said, 'Hallo, Melanie. I've come to see how you are.'

No response.

'You remember me, don't you? Dr Byrd from the English Department. We've all been really worried about you.'

No response.

'Look, I brought you these. I thought they might cheer you up.' She proffered a large, ragged bunch from Lin's garden, wrapped in a supermarket bag.

The bent back hunched into a more obstinately rejecting curve.

'Come on, kiddo, give me a break here,' said Morgan, and freeing the flowers from their Waitrose carrier she laid them across Melanie's lap.

At once Melanie started to rock from side to side, moaning to herself. Her hands clutched at the flowers and began to shred them, tearing the petals from tulips, crushing the starry heads of cow parsley. Morgan put a hand on her shoulder, but Melanie shrugged it off violently, her moans becoming gasping cries. She began to hurl the ruined flowers around the room.

Morgan said, 'Stop it Melanie. Why are you doing this?' The words came out with the rather unconvincing sharpness of someone trying to control a neighbour's unruly child.

In a strangled voice, Melanie said, 'Because there won't be a funeral.'

'What's the matter? What are you talking about?'

'No flowers! No flowers! The baby's dead but there won't be a funeral. They took her away. I wanted her to be dead. I let them kill her.'

'For God's sake, Melanie, what are you saying?'

Melanie's voice rose to a piercing shriek and she began to bang at her head with her clenched fists, repeating over and over again, 'I let them do it, I let them do it, I let them do it,' until a couple of nurses ran in and told Morgan to leave.

Morgan walked back down the corridor and knocked on the psychiatrist's door. She felt unreal, as if the events of the last few minutes had taken place on the other side of a glass screen. The psychiatrist looked up irritably as she came in, clicking the knob of his biro to indicate that he was busy.

Morgan said baldly, 'Melanie told me that she let a baby be killed.'

The psychiatrist sighed with professional impatience. 'I specifically asked you not to mention the kidnapping.'

'I didn't. I gave her some flowers and she started throwing them about and saying she'd let a baby be taken away and killed. She said she wanted it dead.'

'I told you she was in a highly disturbed condition. This is a psychiatric ward, you know.'

Morgan could recognise stalemate when she met it. She said flatly, 'I think she knows what happened to Ben Gilbert. I'm going to phone the police.'

As she closed the door, she noticed with some stray, irrelevant part of her mind that the nameplate said Dr Percival Truelove. In the hospital foyer she dialled 999. She found that her hands were shaking with delayed shock, making it difficult to key in the number. She knew that Dr Truelove might very well be right, that Melanie might simply have been acting out hitherto suppressed feelings of irrational guilt and self-hatred, but it hadn't sounded like that. It had sounded like the truth. A baby had been killed and Melanie had let it happen.

Inspector Burdock, arriving ten minutes later with Sergeant Blossom and WPC Davis, found Dr Truelove disinclined to let Melanie be interviewed.

'We are talking about a very sick girl here, officer. I have to put the needs of my patient first.'

'And I'm talking about a very sick individual at large somewhere in the community,' replied Inspector Burdock stoutly. 'A sick individual who has abducted and possibly killed a young child. I have to follow up every possible lead to find that person. An experienced female officer will talk to Melanie. We won't distress her any more than we have to.'

The interview yielded no results, though. Melanie Wilson had been sedated immediately after her outburst to Dr Byrd, and Mary Blossom, despite her patient efforts, made no headway with her at all. The girl simply stared into space with dazed, dilated eyes and said nothing.

'It's all right, Melanie love, we don't want to scare you. We just want to chat to you a bit. We've heard you're feeling upset about a baby. Is that right? Why don't you tell us about it, love? Did something happen to the baby? Something bad? Just you tell us what you told Dr Byrd about the baby.'

No response. No sign that Melanie had so much as heard the coaxing voice. Her fixed and vacant gaze didn't even flicker. Inspector Burdock left WPC Davis on guard outside the door of Room 6, with instructions to get in touch if there seemed any prospect of making progress, and went downstairs to find Dr Byrd. No problems with articulacy there, at least.

Morgan had looked up Melanie's file before going to the hospital. It had been surprisingly empty of information. Melanie appeared to have no parents or guardian and no address other than her term-time one. She had been a diligent but unnoticeable student, silent in class and putting immense pains into producing competent, colourless essays. There were a couple of medical certificates, one for migraine and the other for glandular fever. Morgan suggested, with a certain malicious pleasure but no real hope of producing further information, that Melanie's personal tutor Rupert Allison might know a bit more about her. As accurately as she could, she reconstructed for Inspector Burdock what Melanie had told her.

'She said a baby was dead but there hadn't been a funeral. She wanted the baby to die and had let it be killed.'

'Any suggestion about who did the killing?'

'She just said "they". She said, "I wanted her to be dead. I let them kill her", and then she started screaming.'

'She talked as if the baby was female? You're quite sure of that?'

'Absolutely certain.'

'But you still got the impression that she could be talking about Ben Gilbert?'

'The psychiatrist seemed to think she was just fantasising, but it sounded real. I could be wrong, though. In fact, perhaps I'm the last person to judge. It was a bit like the mad scene from *Hamlet*, Ophelia chucking her flowers around and talking in code about something rotten in the state of Denmark. Perhaps that predisposed me to believe her. But I was quite certain at the time that she was telling the truth.'

'I remember seeing the film of that when I was a lad,' said Inspector Burdock reflectively. 'Laurence Olivier swooning round the battlements in a blonde wig and a lot of ectoplasm. So is that all you can tell me, Dr Byrd?'

'There's something else,' said Morgan. 'Something that somebody told me. Hang on a minute and it'll come back to me. She had a boyfriend, a student in the philosophy department.' She stopped, as if something had suddenly struck her, and put her hands over her mouth. It seemed to Inspector Burdock that she had turned visibly pale. 'Oh my God, yes, the monkeys. Of course. That's it. Why didn't I think of it before?'

'What exactly are you trying to tell me?'

'Melanie's boyfriend was called Lawrence Craik. He was sent down last term for causing damage to the building where the lab animals are kept.'

Inspector Burdock felt the sober joy of being on the trail at last. 'You don't know the present whereabouts of this Lawrence Craik, by any chance, Dr Byrd?'

'I don't, but the philosophy department will have his home address in their records.'

CHAPTER FOURTEEN

After the delivery of his anonymous letter, Oliver found himself waylaid in the school playground by Cathy and Stephanie, who had already bullied the truth out of the all too pliant Danny. Cathy was tearful and self-pitying, Stephanie blazed with righteous indignation.

'We know all about you, Oliver Cresswell. You're just a stinking rotten telltale and a spy. You told on us to that police lady when all we were doing was playing dollies. And now my dad's stopped my pocket money for a month for going in Hangman's Wood and Cathy's mum slapped her and sent her to bed and it's all your fault. And I'm going to tell the whole school about what you've done and no one will ever speak to you again.'

This threat left Oliver unmoved. Even if he had cared about the possibility of being ostracised, when it came to blackmail he knew he had the upper hand.

He said indifferently, 'Tell who you like. I don't have time to talk to little kids.' He began to walk away, then added devastatingly over his shoulder, 'Anyway, I know what you were doing in that wood and it wasn't playing dollies.'

He felt, with grim satisfaction, that Alka-Seltzer's honour had been salvaged. His violent death at the hands of the mystery intruders would be far harder to avenge. Elspeth would be back soon and perhaps she would help him to do it, since it was obvious that the police didn't care. In the meantime, he had written a careful description of the whole incident on his laptop, including the all-important number of the get-away car.

Oliver was not in the habit of considering anyone's feelings except his own, but the thought of Elspeth made him realise that she would be returning to an empty flat, not even knowing that Alka-Seltzer was dead. For the second time in a week he sat down to compose a letter. This time he wrote laboriously by hand, his tongue thrust into his left cheek as he formed the letters. Oliver disliked his own handwriting, which was clumsy and childish-looking and earned him low marks at school. His pen always seemed to leak a smudge of blue-black ink onto the top joint of his middle finger, and it was hard not to smear the paper. Instinctively, though, he felt that only a hand-written letter would convey the full horror of Alka-Seltzer's death. The right words were hard to find and he had to discard several drafts before he was satisfied. Finally, he put the cap back on his pen and printed out the file called MURDER. He folded up both letter and document and stuffed them into an envelope, then tore his earlier attempts into small pieces before putting them in the wastepaper basket. He didn't trust his mother not to pick them out and read them.

The next day was a Saturday. Morgan was struggling with her belated article when her phone rang. The summer term started on Monday and she could already see that she was going to miss her revised deadline. She felt edgy and unable to concentrate, half her attention drained away by the effort not to think about dead babies. The scene with Melanie had rattled her far more than she had realised at the time. The sudden ringtone made her jump and she found that her hands were sweating slightly as she pulled the phone from her pocket. Whoever was calling her – Inspector Burdock, Rupert Allison, Rosalind Gilbert – she just didn't want to know.

It was Ollie. The sound of his chill, demanding voice was almost a relief.

He said baldly, 'I have to talk to Lin. Mum says I can't come over on my own and she's far too busy to bring me.'

Under other circumstances Morgan might well have replied, 'Tough, kid. We're busy too.' As it was, she said mildly, 'Do you want me to give her a message?'

'I have to talk to her,' said Ollie again. Despite herself, Morgan was aware of the tightness in his voice and the hidden urgency behind it. This was something private, something that mattered.

'OK, hang on a minute. She's taking some paintings to the framer this morning but she may not have left yet. I'll just go and see if she's there.'

Outside, the garden was wind-blown under a racing sky. Morgan picked her way through the tangle of luxuriant growth, ambushed yet again by the memory of Melanie, a demented Ophelia, rocking over a lapful of mutilated flowers. Her arms prickled with sudden goosebumps and she shivered and rolled down her sleeves. Lin was in the studio, meditatively sorting through a stack of canvasses. She was preparing for a big exhibition in London and was more than usually caught up in her work. As always, Morgan tried half-heartedly not to feel excluded by this intense preoccupation with abstract colour and form. As always, the effort failed to pay off. It suddenly seemed a long time since they had really talked.

Ollie's tiger painting was still on its easel in the corner, the great striped beast burning in the jungle gloom above a sinister black box incongruously daubed with coloured blobs. Morgan shivered again at the sight of it, remembering the bright beads strung across Ben Gilbert's abandoned pram. A dead cat. Very possibly a murdered child. The walls of civilisation breached and crumbling and some hideous, unknown thing grinning through the cracks.

Morgan had always prided herself on being too sceptical to believe in premonitions but now she felt her scalp crawl with superstitious dread. What fresh horror was it that was waiting to be revealed? Hastily she delivered Ollie's message and made her way back through the garden as she relayed the answer.

'Lin's just about to load up the van. If you want to go with her, she'll pick you up in half an hour. She thought you might like to choose a frame for that painting of Alka-Seltzer.'

'All right,' said Ollie, cagey and offhand.

So what did I expect, thought Morgan as she went back to her work. Gratitude?

Unlike Morgan, Oliver was wholly untroubled by forebodings. He had never been a superstitious child, and his education, specialised as it had been, had encouraged him to see life simply in terms of problem-solving. Even Elspeth's intensive coaching in the traditions of the Kainu had presented itself to him as a series of challenges to be met and mastered. That was what it meant to be a hunter. His immediate problem, as the battered old van took the road to Oxbourne, was how to deliver his letter to Elspeth's flat while still keeping it a secret even from Lin. They drove without talking, since Lin's hands were occupied with the gears and her eyes with the road ahead, and Oliver took advantage of the companionable silence to formulate a plan.

When they reached their destination, he waited without fidgeting while Lin and the framer, an earnest, bearded man with an over-fastidious, fluting voice, conducted their interminable business. A hunter has to know how to be patient. All the same, he wondered why it took them so long to decide between two almost identical samples of stripped, bleached wood. He himself had spotted the perfect frame for his portrait of Alka-Seltzer as soon as he came into the shop.

When all Lin's canvasses had finally been dealt with, she lifted his picture, still pinned to its drawing-board, onto the counter and indicated that Oliver was the artist. The framer squinted at it with his head on one side, just as he had done with Lin's paintings.

'Hmm, yes. Interesting, very. And what did you have in mind for this, sir?'

'That one,' said Oliver, wasting no words.

The framer raised his eyebrows a little. 'I'm afraid that one would be rather pricey, sir. More than your pocket-money could stretch to, I expect. And possibly a touch too ornate for the picture? How about this one? We've always found it very popular.'

Oliver had never given a thought to picture frames in his life, but now he saw that the boring corner of plain shiny metal made his magnificent tiger look less like a forest creature and more like a zoo one, caged behind bars. The frame that he had chosen, heavy fake bamboo splotched and dappled with black and gold, had something of the dangerous, flickering shadows of the proper jungle. He turned to Lin, his hands and face intently explaining this important point.

Lin nodded. In the loud, flat voice she so seldom used she said, 'We'll have that one. You can add it to my bill.'

Unlike Morgan, she never even noticed that Oliver didn't say thank you. Instead he turned back to the framer. It was already clear that the man had a silly attitude to children and now it was apparent, from some change in his expression, that he believed that Oliver too was deaf. All the better. It is harder to say no to a deaf child.

Deliberately keeping his voice toneless in imitation of Lin's and trying, not altogether successfully, to look appealing, he said, 'Could you possibly do it right away? You see, it's for an old lady whose cat died while she was on holiday. I want her to have it as soon as she gets back.' He stared hard at the man's face as he spoke, like a lip-reader.

Articulating carefully, the framer said, 'I expect we could manage that for you, sir, yes. Come back in an hour.' This time, Oliver thought it would be politic to say thank you.

Lin took him to have elevenses in a café while they waited, and over coke and crisps it was easy to carry out the second half of his plan. He explained, truthfully enough, that he had forgotten to clear away Alka-Seltzer's dishes after he went missing. The cat-food would be growing whiskers by now. If Lin would just drop him off at the campus, he could clear it up and then get the bus home.

Lin had always treated him like a responsible adult and anyway she took other people's business very much at face value. She was too preoccupied with her own world of paint and canvas to do anything else. As he had expected, it never occurred to her to ask if his mother would object to his going home alone. All the same, after he had got out of the van, she paused for a moment to watch him. Even to Lin's dispassionate eye, there was something almost disquieting about the determination with which he trudged off towards the staff residence block, a skinny little figure in blazer and shorts, lugging his tribute to Alka-Seltzer in its outsize brown paper parcel. Poor kid, she thought, with an unexpected flash of concern. It must be hard at his age to be so self-contained about grief.

CHAPTER FIFTEEN

By the time he arrived at 9 Macdonall Close, Inspector
Burdock had already started to build up an impression
of Lawrence Craik. The file reluctantly produced by the
philosophy department had yielded an address in Glasgow and
the information that his parent or guardian was a Ms Morag
Craik who worked in catering. It also contained a handful of
tutors' reports indicating that he was a rather difficult young
man, inclined to be disruptive in seminars, but on further
inquiry, disruptive in this context had turned out to mean
no more than saying in a loud aggressive voice things that his
teachers disagreed with. The lad had never been in any real
trouble prior to the raid on the animal house. The department
had no idea of his present whereabouts but was forwarding
any mail to his home address.

It all added up, Burdock thought. Single parent family,
mother in low-paid employment, clever but resentful youth
emerging from an inner-city comprehensive with a fistful of
exam passes and a chip on his shoulder. The barely controlled

impatience with the pedantry and hair-splitting of university studies and then the discovery of a cause which would channel all his frustration and anger into self-righteous vengeance. The attack on the animal house where Andrew Gilbert's monkeys were kept. Expulsion from the university, further increasing his resentment. And finally, with the help of his weak and depressive girlfriend, the kidnapping of James Gilbert's son.

Inspector Burdock pored again over the smudged and illegible postmark on the anonymous letter purporting to come from the kidnapper. Glasgow was a name with about the right number of letters, and the first one looked as if it might possibly be a G. Not that Lawrence Craik could plausibly be concealing little Ben Gilbert in his mother's tenement flat. But then, if Melanie Wilson was to be believed, little Ben Gilbert was already dead.

In the event, Macdonall Close proved to be neither a tenement nor a tower block but a cul-de-sac of Edwardian houses, solidly built from good local sandstone and nicely renovated, their gardens full of fancy paving and dwarf conifers and plants in terracotta pots. Outside number nine a neat green van was parked, with GREENFEASTS: VEGAN PARTY CATERING painted in gold letters on its glossy side.

The woman who opened the door was equally far from Inspector Burdock's preconceptions about Lawrence Craik's mother. She was tall and rather elegant in a negligent, effortless way, as if she bought her clothes from Oxfam shops but put them together with flair. Her hair must once have been red before it faded to the colour of silver sand and she had sharply intelligent eyes in a worn but still handsome face. She seemed completely unperturbed by the sudden arrival of a detective chief inspector to interview her son in connection with a missing child.

'Yes, Lawrie's here. You're lucky to catch him. He only got back last night. Up the stairs and first door on the right. I'll be in the kitchen if you need me.'

Inspector Burdock padded slowly up the staircase, subliminally noting its display of social markers – stripped pine banisters, sisal matting, framed posters of endangered species – while he chewed thoughtfully over the information he had just been given. Lawrence Craik had been away from Glasgow, away for some time by the sound of it. Burdock felt his nostrils twitch with anticipation. After so many days of frustration and false leads, at last he was really on the scent.

Lawrence Craik's study bedroom was large and airy. Yet more ecological posters were thumb-tacked to the walls, angrier posters with sharp, aggressive slogans, and there was a large map of Scotland hanging above the desk. Lawrence Craik himself was sitting in front of an impressive-looking laptop (not a MacBock, Burdock noted) tinkering with a complicated graph. He turned his head inquiringly as the door opened.

He was a wiry-looking, red-haired youth, thin-skinned and freckled, whose narrow green eyes focused on his unexpected visitor with the smouldering intensity of a compulsive scholar, a fanatic, a martyr. Burdock's nose twitched again. His other predictions might have been wide of the mark, but this intransigent face fitted the bill exactly.

'Detective Chief Inspector Burdock,' he said formally. 'I take it you are Lawrence Craik. I'm going to have to ask you a few questions relating to the kidnapping of Benjamin Gilbert.'

The red-headed youth rummaged among the papers on his desk, found a pair of wire-rimmed spectacles and jammed them on his nose. His short-sighted frown was replaced by a stare of frank bewilderment as he asked, 'Benjamin who? Never heard of him.'

Equally taken aback, Burdock answered the question with one of his own. 'Where on earth have you been hiding for the last few weeks then, lad? You must be the only person in the country who hasn't.'

Lawrence Craik stabbed a finger at the top left-hand corner of the map. 'St Kilda,' he said. 'I'm helping with a nature conservancy project, monitoring the bird life. There's no internet or phone reception, so we tend to get a bit out of touch. I've come home for a few days to write up my notes and get my mum to wash my socks.'

His voice was light and friendly, what Burdock thought of as an educated voice despite its strong Scottish tang. His alibi would have to be checked out, of course, but it sounded as cast-iron as a ship's boiler. Almost too cast-iron, if anything.

Unwilling to be deflected, Burdock ploughed firmly on. 'I have reason to believe you know a Melanie Wilson. I gather she's a girlfriend of yours.'

A look of alarm flashed over the boy's face. 'Is Melanie all right?'

'If you would just answer the question, lad.'

'Yes, I know Melanie Wilson, Inspector, and no, she's not my girlfriend. She's my sister. Now would you kindly tell me what's happened to her.'

'Your sister, you say? I thought she hadn't any family.'

'My foster-sister. When I was about fifteen, Mum decided I was a bit too privileged, what with being an only child and everything. Melanie didn't live with us all that long, but we managed to stay in touch. That's why I went to Oxbourne University. Big mistake, as it turned out.'

'You mean because you were sent down?'

'I mean because philosophy turned out to be a total arse-aching waste of time. I was glad when they chucked me out. Look, what is all this anyway?'

Inspector Burdock said quietly, 'Benjamin Gilbert is the infant son of James and Libby Gilbert. He was kidnapped

123

three weeks ago. Melanie Wilson was au pairing for them at the time.'

The scowl had returned to Lawrence Craik's brow. 'So you're accusing Melanie of taking him?'

'I'm attempting to establish the facts. We know she couldn't have done it on her own.'

'What exactly are you getting at, Inspector?'

'James Gilbert is the brother of Dr Andrew Gilbert. I gather you took exception to his animal experiments.'

'I was trying to stop a crime from being committed. You should understand that, Inspector. It's your job too, isn't it?'

Burdock said stolidly, 'It's my job to uphold the law.'

'Even if the law lets innocent creatures be tortured and killed?'

'You could say that Ben Gilbert is an innocent creature too.'

Lawrence Craik pushed back his chair and jumped to his feet, his face so contorted with sudden rage that his eyes had vanished into furious slits. 'You think that anyone who cares about cruelty to animals is bound to go round torturing babies. Well, you can think again, mister. For the last six weeks I've been marooned on a lump of rock in the middle of the Atlantic, so you'll just have to find somebody else to stitch up.'

Burdock took out a folded piece of paper and handed it over. He said grimly, 'Not everyone is so squeamish about torturing babies. Does this mean anything to you?' He watched the young man's face as he opened it and read the single brutal sentence.

'Christ, that's revolting.'

Burdock said implacably, 'That's a copy of a letter that someone sent to Ben Gilbert's parents. And Melanie talked about letting a baby be killed. If you want to protect the innocent, you can stop being so bloody paranoid and answer my questions.'

Lawrence Craik stared at the paper for a long time. Finally he muttered, 'If the baby's been hurt then it wasn't Melanie that took him.'

'Exactly what are you telling me, lad? That she might have taken a baby, but she wouldn't harm it?'

The boy shook his head. 'I'm sorry. I can't answer that.'

'You can't or you're not prepared to?'

'Look, get someone sympathetic to talk to Melanie. She needs help, not interrogation in some stinking police cell.'

'You've got a vivid imagination, lad, I'll say that. We can't talk to Melanie. She's in hospital.'

If Burdock had expected to provoke another outburst he failed, but he was not disappointed. Lawrence Craik's lack of shock at the news told its own story. He was silent for a moment, then he asked quietly, 'What happened this time?'

'Overdose. Don't worry, they found her in time, but she isn't in any state to talk. So I could do with a bit of co-operation from you, lad.'

'I've already told you. There's nothing I can say.'

Burdock said wearily, 'All right, we'll leave it there for the time being.' He went downstairs to tackle the mother, but Ms Craik, though considerably more gracious about it, proved as uncommunicative as her son.

'I'm afraid Lawrie can be rather hasty, and of course he's always been terribly protective of Melanie, but I think this time he's right. You can't expect him to pass on things that Melanie told him in confidence, and I really don't feel that I should either. I doubt if it would help in any case. I could put you in touch with her social worker if you like. Now can I make you a cup of tea before you go?

The kitchen smelt pleasantly of home-made biscuits and Burdock's throat was dry. However, before the kettle came to the boil his phone began to vibrate.

'Inspector Burdock here. Yes. What? No, not a dicky-bird. Oh my God, not him again. He's found *what*? Jesus, that's all we didn't need. Right, you carry on, Crewe. I'll get there as soon as I can.'

CHAPTER SIXTEEN

Oliver propped the painting of Alka-Seltzer against his bare knees and fished about in his pocket for the door-key. It seemed like months rather than weeks since he had last been to Elspeth's flat, months of frustration and non-stop adult surveillance. He felt a sense of relief, almost of homecoming, mixed with the sadness of knowing that there was no battle-scarred old tomcat waiting for him inside. But the tribal masks and spears would still be there, and that congenial atmosphere of books and clutter and dust, so different from the pretentiously flouncy spickness that his mother went in for.

He got the door open and manhandled the heavy painting inside, propping it up against the legs of the hall table. There was an untidy pile of brown envelopes on top. Oliver pulled out his own letter to Elspeth and added it to the heap, then went through to the kitchen to clear away Alka-Seltzer's dishes.

But someone else had already had the same idea. The dishes had been neatly licked clean of meat and milk, and muddy cat footprints on the kitchen lino showed that the intruder had been a much smaller animal than Alka-Seltzer. It had been a tomcat, though. You could smell where it had left its mark, claiming Alka-Seltzer's territory as its own. Oliver clenched his fists. For a moment he felt quite helpless with rage and grief. It was as if jackals had gathered at the feeding-place of a dead lion.

No, not a lion. A tiger. A tiger still burning brightly even in the night-dark forest of death. Alka-Seltzer was an ancestor spirit now, like the Kainu spirits Elspeth had told him about. His own painting of the dead cat was like an ancestor mask, those masks which decorated the end-poles of the huts in the photographs of the forest which Elspeth had shown him. The thing to do was to hang up the picture; then the spirit of Alka-Seltzer would extend his power over Elspeth and her house. Oliver rooted around in the cupboard where Elspeth kept her tools and found a hammer and a tin of assorted nails. Over the study desk would be the best place, he decided.

When he tried to open the study door, something resisted the pressure. He had to push quite hard and then almost tripped over the tangled mess inside, where an open suitcase had strewn its contents over the floor. All the drawers of the desk had been pulled out as well. Puzzled, Oliver came further into the room. Round the corner of the desk he glimpsed something lying huddled like a heap of old clothes. Quite slowly and calmly he walked up to it. Her eyes were open, but he knew at once that she was dead. Alka-Seltzer's head had lolled on the blue cot blanket at just the same unnatural angle.

For once, Morgan's writing was going rather well. As occasionally but all too rarely happened, she could sense the potential shape of exciting new ideas forming somewhere in the recesses of her mind. She had only to go with the flow and she would capture them. She was too intent on her elusive prey to notice when her phone started to ring. As usual, she had forgotten to switch it off. When the sound did finally penetrate her consciousness, she almost decided to ignore it. She knew from bitter past experience that at this stage any break in her concentration would be fatal. It was the persistence of the ringing which finally forced her to pick up the phone. It sounded like an emergency, and sure enough it was. She heard Ollie's voice, flat and chill, saying without preamble, 'Elspeth is dead.'

Whatever disaster Morgan had expected, it was not this. She had noticed in the past that when you hit people with the news of an unexpected death, the first word they tend to say is 'Shit!' She said it now. For a moment Ollie's tone had carried absolute conviction, followed almost at once by near disbelief.

'Ollie, are you sure? How do you know?'

'I'm in her flat. I found her. She's lying on the floor. She's dead.'

'Are you sure? Look, shouldn't we phone for an ambulance?'

Ollie's voice began to get shriller, as if he was on the verge of losing control. 'She's dead. I know she is. She's really, really dead. Her head's all sideways like Alka-Seltzer's was. And she's cold. I touched her.'

'All right, all right, I believe you. Look, you'd better go and find Collington. Stay with him till I get there. I'll be as quick as I can.'

Ollie said with devastating politeness, 'Actually, I'd rather stay here, thanks,' and rang off.

Morgan dialled 999 for a possibly redundant ambulance and shut her laptop. A minute later it occurred to her that she had forgotten to save her day's work, but by then she had already grabbed her keys from the kitchen dresser and was out of the house and running towards the car. It didn't matter anyway. Whatever the possible developments she had dimly glimpsed, she knew they were gone for good. She had never taken the winding road to Oxbourne so fast. Speeding through Hangman's Wood, she suddenly remembered her premonition of earlier in the day and felt that mixture of annoyance and alarm which takes hold of a convinced rationalist whenever a palpable superstition appears to have evidence on its side.

It was a coincidence, for Christ's sake. She didn't believe in premonitions.

The door of Elspeth's flat was unlocked. Morgan pushed it open and went in. The staff accommodation block was modern and purpose-built, and Elspeth had never bothered to change the cream paint and beige cord carpet, but nevertheless she had managed to impress her formidable personality on the blandness of the decor. The hall smelt ancient and indefinably foreign, an effect to which Alka-Seltzer had contributed his own pungent note. A fan of spears hung above the hall table while a carved mask and various unidentifiable but somehow sinister objects decorated the opposite wall. The floor was littered with brown paper as if someone had been unwrapping a parcel.

Morgan shouted, 'Ollie, where are you?' and heard him call out wordlessly in reply. She walked to the end of the passage and opened the study door. The room had been ransacked: papers and other possessions flung around in brutal confusion. Morgan picked her way into the room and found Elspeth's body, lying just as Ollie had described it. Though the waxen flesh and the wry neck made it an empty gesture, she went down on her knees and uselessly felt for the non-existent pulse. Ollie was right, Elspeth was really dead. Ollie himself was standing by the window. His face was pale and exhausted, and it had a scrubbed look, as if he had recently washed away

131

tears. His portrait of Alka-Seltzer, in an imposing black and gold frame, had been propped up against a nearby bookcase. Whether because of the frame or because of its proximity to the corpse, the painting seemed to have acquired a new and baleful power.

Ollie said, in a surprisingly adult voice, 'She's been murdered, hasn't she? Someone searched the flat and murdered her.' Remembering his violent reaction to Alka-Seltzer's death, Morgan was struck by how calm he sounded.

'It certainly looks that way. She must have come back and disturbed the burglars. Though what they can have wanted to steal ... OK, we'd better phone the police, or have you done that already?'

Ollie shook his head. 'I thought it would come better from a grown-up.'

'Check. Now, you go and put the kettle on and see if you can rustle us up a hot drink.'

By the time both the ambulance and the police arrived, Morgan and Ollie were sitting at the kitchen table drinking rather nasty instant coffee. Morgan had made sure that Ollie's mug had several spoonfuls of sugar stirred into it. Though he seemed so self-possessed, she suspected that he was far more disturbed by what had happened than he wanted to let her see. He had a peaky, transparent look and he was clasping the hot mug with both hands to prevent himself from shivering.

Morgan herself felt numb, as if the sheer grotesqueness of Elspeth's death had dislocated her from reality. It was a relief when the doorbell rang and the bustle and procedure of a police investigation could begin.

Mary Blossom was universally thought to have a gift for relating to kids, another way of saying that as a female officer she invariably got landed with them. While the pathologist and the photographer busied themselves with the corpse, she interviewed the small boy who had found it, a curiously detached and evasive witness and one she found difficult to warm to.

'Let's start with your name, shall we?'

'Oliver Cresswell.'

'All right, Oliver, can you tell me exactly what happened? You came here to visit Dr Blair-Guthrie?'

'Not exactly. I thought she was still away. I had a key, you see, because I'd been feeding Alka-Seltzer. Her cat. But then he got killed.'

'So what were you doing here?'

'I came to bring her a painting I did.'

'A sort of welcome home present?'

'Not exactly.'

'Could anybody else have got their hands on that key of yours? Did you ever leave it lying around?'

'It was always in my inside blazer pocket. It has a zip.'

'OK, so you let yourself in with your key, and then what happened?'

'I went into the kitchen first. I was going to hang the picture up so I needed a hammer. Then I went into the study and she was just lying there.'

'And what time was this?'

'I suppose about half past twelve.'

'But that was nearly three hours ago. Why didn't you report it right away?'

'I don't know.'

'What were you doing all that time?'

'I talked to her a bit, I suppose.'

'Did you touch anything, move anything?'

'Only her hand. I touched her hand.'

Mary Blossom looked speculatively at the boy and he stared impassively back at her with pale, unblinking eyes. She was certain that he was hiding something, something that he believed to be important.

'And that's all you know about what happened?'

With sudden urgency the boy said, 'You ought to look for the men who kidnapped Alka-Seltzer. The men in the blue BMW.'

Mary Blossom relaxed. What young Oliver was hiding was probably only a cops and robbers fantasy. She said kindly,

'A blue BMW, eh? We'll bear that in mind, don't you worry. OK, Oliver, I'm going to ask Dr Byrd to take you home now, but we'll probably want to talk to you again.'

Once Morgan and Oliver had gone, she went to find Sergeant Crewe who was sifting patiently through the debris in the study while the photographer fidgeted round the corpse with his tripod and lights.

'The kid was holding out on me about something, but I don't reckon it matters. Looks like an open and shut case, doesn't it. A burglary that went wrong.'

'I wouldn't bank on it, Cherry. Take a gander at this.' He handed her a rectangle of cardboard with a photograph glued to it, the back view of a stark-naked small boy standing stiffly to attention. Someone had taken a scalpel to the picture and cut a neat series of nicks across the shoulders and back. Mary Blossom whistled.

'Turn it over,' said Crewe grimly. On the other side of the card the naked child stood facing the camera, his expression stern and emotionless and his cheekbones painted with a pattern of swirling dots. There was a dark reddish thumbprint on the photograph which looked nastily like blood. It had been splodged down onto the child's forehead, and the features underneath it were unmistakably those of young Oliver Cresswell.

'Oh Jesus!' said Mary Blossom. 'Satanic abuse. That's all we bleeding well need!'

Morgan too had been observing Ollie closely. At first they drove in silence, locked in their separate thoughts, but presently she said, 'There was something you weren't letting on about just now.'

Ollie slid his eyes sideways towards her and said nothing.

Morgan said irritably, 'Oh come on, kid, this is a murder investigation, for Christ's sake. It isn't a game.'

Ollie's pale, secretive face flamed with sudden indignation. He said, 'I'm not playing games and I'm not a bloody kid!' His voice was shaking with rage and he seemed on the brink of tears.

'OK, OK,' Morgan said soothingly, 'I believe you.'

'No you bloody don't! Nobody bloody believes me! You heard that police-lady just now. "We'll bear it in mind, Oliver dear. Now run along home and play".'

'The men in the blue BMW,' said Morgan, remembering. 'Those were the ones who kidnapped Alka-Seltzer, right?' Like Sergeant Blossom, she was unable to keep the scepticism out of her voice.

With chilly dignity, Ollie said, 'You think I'm just making it up, but I'm not. I know what happened. I know why Elspeth was killed.'

Morgan looked at him curiously and he stared coldly back. She said, 'I didn't mean it like that. I'm sorry. Like to tell me about it?'

'I wouldn't, actually,' said Ollie grandly. 'I need to get some expert advice first.'

'Expert advice, yet! What sort of expert advice?'

Suddenly conciliatory, the boy said, 'Look, I need to send a letter and I don't want Mum to know. Can I come back to your house and write it?'

Hunched over a notepad at the kitchen table, Ollie composed his letter with one arm crooked round the paper to shield it from view. Morgan busied herself at the sink and tactfully refrained from looking at him. Finally, Ollie licked the flap of the envelope, banged it down and slid his missive across the table to her. It was addressed, in large untidy script, to Torquil Guthrie MP, House of Commons, London and Ollie had added, in emphatic capitals, EXTREAMLY IMPORTANT!!! He had underlined it twice.

He studied Morgan's face as she read it and said tensely, 'It needs to be posted right away.'

'OK, I'll do it now. Look, why don't you go and talk to Lin? She's in the painting shed.'

Ollie hesitated. 'Does she know about Elspeth?'

'Not yet. Want me to come with you?'

Ollie shook his head. 'It's all right. I'll tell her.'

Morgan dropped her hand onto his shoulder for a moment, making it seem accidental. She said, 'You were fond of Elspeth, weren't you, kid?'

Drawing himself up to his full four and a half feet, Ollie said in his most arrogant voice, 'I had a high opinion of her. She was an extremely intelligent person.'

'I know,' said Morgan quietly. 'I'm going to miss her too.'

CHAPTER SEVENTEEN

By the time Inspector Burdock arrived at the scene of the crime, the initial bustle of activity had already subsided. The corpse had been removed, with only an outline of tape tacked to the carpet to mark where it had lain, and the pathologist and the photographer had long since packed up and gone home. Only Sergeant Crewe and Sergeant Blossom remained, taking a welcome break in Dr Blair-Guthrie's kitchen over a mug of tea and a take-away.

'Evening, sir,' said Mary Blossom solicitously. 'Care for a slice of pizza?'

'I wouldn't say no, Sergeant. Any more tea in that pot?'

'Reckon I can squeeze you out a cup, sir.'

'All right then, what have we got? I take it the old girl came home and disturbed an intruder. Any clues as to who it was?'

'Oh, there are *clues* all right, sir,' said Sergeant Crewe in a meaningful voice. 'Proper old murder mystery we have here and no mistake. Like to take a look?' He slid a bulging folder in front of Inspector Burdock. 'This one's the prize exhibit. Nasty, eh? And the other side is even nastier.'

Burdock flipped the photograph over. 'Good God, that's young Oliver Cresswell. Didn't you say he found the body?'

'So he claims.'

'Something pretty unhealthy going on there, by the look of it. Child abuse with fancy trimmings – every copper's nightmare. Tabloid headlines, public hysteria, the whole messy works.'

'Let's hope not, sir. And these were on the hall table.' 'These' were a pile of envelopes. Burdock looked a question. 'A missive from young Sherlock to the victim, spinning some yarn about that cat we found in the pram, plus a whole heap from a religious maniac,' said Crewe, wooden faced.

Burdock picked up the top letter on the pile. Cheap brown envelope, old-fashioned loopy script, posted second-class the previous week in central London. The message inside had neither address nor signature. It was written painstakingly in red ink on a yellowing page torn from an exercise book.

A BASTARD shall not enter into the congregation of THE LORD.

WOE unto them that call EVIL good and take away the righteousness of the righteous. As FIRE devoureth the stubble and the FLAME consumeth the chaff, so their root shall be as rottenness and their blossom shall go up as dust.

And she DEPARTED and wandered in the wilderness of Beersheba. For she said, Let me not see THE DEATH OF THE CHILD, and she sat over against him and lift up her voice and wept.

'Jesus, Mary and Joseph!' said Burdock mildly but with feeling. 'Are all the rest like that?'

'Pretty much, sir, yes. But the really interesting thing is the postmarks. Our biblical pen-pal began sending off these thoughts for the day just three days after Ben Gilbert went missing.'

Inspector Burdock glanced back at the paper in his hand. 'She said, let me not see the death of the child,' he read slowly.

Mary Blossom met his eye and nodded. 'You thinking what I am, sir? Sounds as if he could be talking about Melanie Wilson.'

By the following afternoon Burdock had questioned half the occupants of the staff accommodation block and ascertained that the other half had not yet returned from wherever it is that dedicated scholars disappear to in the university vacation. Nobody had noticed a thing. Burdock relieved his frustration by sounding off to Sergeant Crewe about the wasting of taxpayers' money on a load of unobservant eggheads.

Mary Blossom had been dispatched to Glasgow first thing that morning with instructions to ingratiate herself with Melanie Wilson's social worker.

'I want off the record information and I want it today. Convince her there isn't time to go through official channels if we're to find that baby alive.'

Mary Blossom gave him a direct look. 'Still think there's any chance of that, sir?'

'Too early to say yet, Sergeant,' replied Burdock stiffly. He knew she shared his conviction that Ben Gilbert was dead.

Now he was sitting at his desk with Sergeant Crewe's collection of clues spread out in front of him. Burdock looked at them with irritation. Clues were all very fine in a murder mystery; in a real investigation what you needed was evidence, and there seemed to be precious little of that so far. Crewe himself was facing him across the desk with a trustingly doggy look as if only waiting for a suggestion about how to proceed before dashing off and doing something useful. Burdock tugged thoughtfully at his walrus moustache, pulled a notepad towards him and scratched his head with the end of his biro.

'OK, we have one kidnapping and one murder, possibly two. The simplest hypothesis is that there is no connection. Let's say that Melanie Wilson took the baby, with the assistance of person or persons unknown, and Dr Blair-Guthrie walked in on a burglar who panicked and killed her. So we need to check up on likely local housebreakers and examine the flat again from that angle. How did he get in, did he leave any traces, did he take anything and, if so, has he tried to flog it to anyone?

'On the other hand, the two crimes may be connected in some way. So what have we got?'

He scribbled a short list of names on his notepad.

Lawrence Craik
Melanie Wilson
letter-writer – anon (1)
letter-writer – anon (2)
Oliver Cresswell

'Neither of the first two could have killed Dr Blair-Guthrie but Lawrence Craik may well have master-minded the kidnap. He reacted very violently when I questioned him about it. Suggested I was trying to set him up. And if that is the case, it's possible he may know something about the murder as well.

'If the baby was taken with Melanie's connivance, she probably didn't intend the kidnapper to kill it. Supposing he did, that is. But she almost certainly knows his identity. The only problem is getting it out of her.

'Our first letter-writer may be a hoaxer or he may know something. If it was Lawrence Craik, he got somebody else to post it. We need to find the rest of Craik's animal liberationist chums.

'Letter-writer number two may be a red herring, but he sounds as if he knows about Melanie and the baby. So we need to find out if she had got involved with some fringe religious group. She sounds just the type who might. She may even have confessed to our unknown correspondent about her part in the kidnapping.'

'Seal of the confessional stuff, you mean, sir?'

'Something like that. So we need to find him and get him to talk. Come to that, we need to find out why he was writing to Dr Blair-Guthrie. And then there's young Oliver. That's a tricky one. He found Ben Gilbert's pram. He found Dr Blair-Guthrie's body. He seems to be involved in some sort of unwholesome hanky-panky. He may well know something he's not letting on about.'

'Cherry reckoned he was hiding something, sir. On the other hand, he seems to have a powerful imagination. Dreamed up that far-fetched plot about catnapping villains. And he put a picture he painted next to the body – sort of fierce great tiger affair. Perhaps he put the photograph there as well. It could be part of some game he's playing.'

'Just possibly. Or it could be something else. And in that case we need to know whether Dr Blair-Guthrie was involved.'

'There was some nasty stuff hung up in that flat of hers.'

'She was an anthropologist, Crewe. Studied savages. She'd have collected that sort of thing. Still, you never know. We need to find out a bit more about her. Come to that, we need a formal identification of the body.'

'What about Dr Byrd? She was a friend of the deceased and she knows young Oliver too. And I tell you what, sir ...'

'Yes, Crewe?'

'Her subject's Eng Lit. You should show her those letters. She might make something of them.'

'I thought Eng Lit was poems and stuff. Nice thoughts about daffs.'

'Not anymore, sir. Now it's all post-structuralism and, what do they call it now, deconstruction. I saw a piece about it on the telly the other night. Sort of decoding, it is, apparently. Sussing out the text for hidden clues. If our religious friend is trying to tell us something, Dr Byrd might have a notion what it is.'

Morgan had not expected to be disturbed by identifying Elspeth's body; after all, she had already seen it and touched it. But when the sheet was folded back in the mortuary and she saw the stern, craggy face with its proudly jutting nose, she realised that yesterday's tumbled corpse had been composed into something as distant and formal as if it had been carved from stone. This was no longer the woman she had known, or rather it was some fierce and private essence of her become visible at last but untouchable. Morgan reached out a hand as if to stroke the rough frizz of white hair, then let it fall to her side, rebuked by the austerity of death. She turned away, not wanting to see the sheet pulled back over that silent face.

'Yes, that is Elspeth Blair-Guthrie.'

Inspector Burdock took her by the elbow and led her out into the corridor. She was surprised to find herself grateful for his steering hand.

'Sorry. It was a shock, I don't know why.' Morgan thought of herself as someone who didn't cry, ever. She wasn't crying now, she was shivering the way Ollie had done the previous day. She said, 'I'll be all right in a minute,' and tried to stop her teeth from chattering.

She was still shivering when they got back to the police station. Inspector Burdock was presumably used to dealing with the emotional reactions of bystanders to sudden and violent death. He said briskly, 'Come up to my office and sit down. I'll get them to bring you some tea.'

The tea came in a thick white mug. It was hot and stewed and very sweet. It helped. It helped too that Inspector Burdock wanted her to talk about Elspeth. Morgan found she badly needed to reconstruct the living person that Elspeth had been.

'What do you want me to tell you?'

'I'd like to get a general sense of her character to start with.'

'Tough. Strong. Forthright. Honest. She had a genius for getting people to talk. Rainforest Indians, closed religious sects, anyone. A good teacher, especially with bright students. Superficially eccentric. Formidably intelligent, though nowadays her scholarship would be dismissed as out of date. Kind. I had a lot of respect for her.' Morgan realised as she spoke that she was using almost the same words as Ollie had done yesterday and for the same reason. Neither of them had the guts to say out loud 'I loved her'.

'Would anyone have had a reason to kill her?'

'Not in Oxbourne, I wouldn't have thought. She wasn't a person who made enemies, though she could certainly speak her mind. She didn't suffer fools gladly. She did nearly get killed once years ago in South America when gold prospectors and government troops attacked a tribe she was studying.'

'Did she have any family?'

'Five or six brothers and sisters, but they're all dead now. She was the youngest by at least a decade. She used to say that growing up as part of a tribe was what made her an anthropologist. I think her father was a baronet or something like that. She was Torquil Guthrie's aunt – I think they were quite close.'

Inspector Burdock looked puzzled. 'Should I have heard of him?'

'You know, the maverick MP – lost causes and tartan politics.'

'You mean he's a Scottish Nationalist?'

'Deep green politics with a thin red stripe running through them. He used to be environment spokesman for the Liberal Democrats until he fell out with them during their coalition with the Tories.'

Morgan had been wondering uneasily if she ought to mention Ollie's letter. Now she realised that she wasn't going to. Whatever Ollie was up to, she would leave him to get on with it. Without being aware of it, she had decided overnight that he knew what he was doing.

As if he had read her thoughts, Inspector Burdock asked, 'What about young Oliver Cresswell? I gather you know him quite well.'

'Ollie? He's a bit of an oddity. A loner. His mother's bringing him up to be a genius and it hasn't done him any favours. But he's very much his own person.'

'Would you say he had a vivid imagination?'

'For mathematical concepts, perhaps. He's not the sort of kid that plays at cops and robbers.'

Burdock eyed her warily, then seemed to come to a decision. 'Look, this is completely confidential, but we think he may have been involved in some kind of satanic abuse. Do you think there's any possibility that Dr Blair-Guthrie could have been a party to that in some way?'

'I think it wholly improbable. Anyway, I thought satanic abuse was supposed to be a myth.'

'You mean she was an old-fashioned maiden lady?'

Elspeth had been a pioneering lesbian activist long before Morgan was born, but she judged it would be wiser not to say so. What to her was a proof of admirable moral courage might strike the inspector rather differently and this didn't seem the moment to come out and be counted. Instead she said, 'Well, hardly, but she was an extremely balanced and rational person.'

'You mentioned a connection with religious cults.'

'She was an anthropologist. She did a study of a sect called the Sealed Brethren – a classic of its kind, I believe. But that doesn't mean she went in for witches' sabbaths.'

'Supposing young Oliver were in any sort of trouble, who would he be likely to turn to?'

'He might tell Lin – my partner – but I think I would know if he had. Elspeth was the only other person he trusted. You think he may have confided in her and she tried to tackle the abuser? It's possible. She was a very brave woman. What are you going to do about it?'

'I haven't decided yet.'

'Well, I'd tread delicately if I were you. Mrs Cresswell's an impossible person, and she's liable to have hysterics at the mere suggestion. If you're not careful, the poor kid is going to end up seethed in his mother's milk.'

'I was thinking we might arrange for a child psychologist to see him. I'm pretty sure he knows more than he's telling us. It's even possible that he knows who caused Dr Blair-Guthrie's death.'

Morgan gave him a sidelong glance. 'Yes, he just might at that. It's worth a try. Though you won't get much change out of Ollie if he doesn't want to tell.'

Burdock thought her an odd woman, brusque and spiky and somehow unfeminine despite her striking looks, as if there were signals that she was refusing to send out. Perhaps it was just that she wore her hair so short. He liked her, though. She was direct and perceptive, and she had given him some useful information. She seemed to have recovered from her distress in the mortuary; he had wondered for a moment if she was going to faint, though she didn't seem at all the fainting type. She was certainly the talking type though. Real way with words, Burdock thought, but then you'd expect that, of course, with her being an expert in Eng Lit. Rather hesitantly, he outlined Sergeant Crewe's suggestion.

Morgan laughed. 'Post-structuralism is a bit out of date these days, Inspector, but I'll take a look if you like.' She proved to be a fast reader, zipping attentively through the sheaf of letters.

Burdock said, 'There seem to be references to the missing baby. Do you think Melanie Wilson could have joined some kind of religious group?'

Morgan said slowly, 'She could, students often do, but it tends to be terribly gregarious and evangelical. This is something solitary. Obsessive. And the writer is middle-aged or elderly, probably poorly educated. You can see it in the handwriting. And whoever it is knows the Old Testament back to front which Christian students never do in my experience. And it's the King James version. Any group Melanie might join would use the Good News Bible. No, this is something different. It means something, though – your Sergeant Crewe is right about that. It's not just random texts. There's a code here all right but I don't think I can crack it for you. There's something – no, it's gone.'

'Ah well, never mind,' said Burdock philosophically. 'At least you've given me a bit of a lead.'

'It may well have nothing to do with the Gilbert baby at all, you know. I told you Elspeth was interested in closed sects. This correspondence was probably part of her fieldwork.'

'You've been a great help, Dr Byrd,' Burdock said formally, bringing the interview to a close. 'If you think of anything else that might be relevant, let us know.'

'I'll do that, yes,' said Morgan abruptly, getting to her feet. 'Just find the bastard who killed Elspeth before I do, if you don't want another murder on your hands.'

CHAPTER EIGHTEEN

Mary Blossom had had a long day. Catching the train to Glasgow had meant early rising, a snatched breakfast and a lengthy wait in Birmingham station. By the time she reported back at the end of the afternoon she felt weary and crumpled and in need of refreshment, but that was not what struck Inspector Burdock when she walked into his office.

'You look like the cat that got the canary, Sergeant. I take it you've found something?'

'Well it could be just another false lead, sir, but yes, I think we might be in business.'

Melanie Wilson's social worker had turned out to be friendly and forthcoming, a brisk, sensible woman about Mary Blossom's age and very much her sort of person. Melanie had been one of her first clients and she still felt concerned about her. She had needed little prompting to tell what she knew. Melanie's mother had remarried when her daughter was less than a year old, a smooth-talking, superficially charming chancer called Eddie McBride who had proved to be both a petty criminal and a drunk. It was only when Melanie had fainted in the school gym, aged thirteen, and had been found to be four months pregnant that anyone outside the family circle realised that he was also a child abuser. He had started interfering with Melanie when she was three and had been raping her nightly since she was ten, almost certainly with her mother's tacit consent.

'McBride was a sadist on the quiet, used to beat his wife up but not so it showed. I think she let him have Melanie for the sake of peace and quiet. There was a wee brother, too, who may also have been molested, but he was much too young to testify. He wasn't McBride's child – the mother used to walk out from time to time and find a fancy man, but McBride always sweet-talked her back. It was after they got back together again the first time that he started abusing Melanie. The mother was so downtrodden by the time the case came to court that she would have walked off a cliff if McBride had told her to. He got seven years in the end, which is mild compared to what I'd have given him.'

After the abortion, Melanie had been fostered by Lawrence Craik's mother who had found herself unable to cope with the girl's anorexia and worsening depression. A lengthy period as an in-patient had been followed by several further foster homes.

'But she was always bright, good at her books. Too good if anything, if you get my meaning. She'd spend hours doing her homework, wanting to have everything perfect. It was like the eating problem, really, a need to be in control. And she was determined to win a place at college and get out of Glasgow. I think she was always afraid that McBride might come back.'

When Mary Blossom had given him the gist of what she had learnt, Inspector Burdock scratched his head thoughtfully and considered it.

'So Melanie Wilson fits the classic profile of a baby-snatcher. Insecure, obsessive, traumatic abortion in her early teens. But would she have helped somebody else to do it?'

'I've been thinking about that, sir. Suppose whoever persuaded her to help him take the baby gave her the idea she could keep it. And then she found out her mistake.'

'And that someone could have been Lawrence Craik, who knew her history, though he would have needed an accomplice. But if we're right about what may have happened to Oliver Cresswell, it sounds as if we ought to check out McBride.'

'Oh I've already done that, sir. He was in Barlinnie, but apparently they let him out last year. Glasgow CID are sending us a photograph. Bit out of date, but the best they can do.'

'Then the sooner we get some sense out of young Oliver the better. So before you knock off for the night, you can come and help me talk to Mrs Cresswell.'

'Does it take two? I'm really knackered. I was up at six this morning and I'm dying to put my feet up.'

'According to Dr Byrd, she's a hysterical woman who needs to be handled with kid gloves.'

'Won't Crewe's kid gloves do, sir?'

'If you enrol for a man's job, Sergeant, you have to be prepared to supply a woman's touch. You've done well, by the way. There's time for a bite to eat before we go.'

Mrs Cresswell proved to be a carefully made-up woman in her early fifties whose plump, petulant face showed the signs of discreet cosmetic surgery. She allowed them into her house with grudging suspicion, but no further than the hall, which had elaborate chintz drapes, ankle-deep carpeting and walls rag-rolled in pink. Somewhere in the background, a solo violin was playing something tricky but austere. Inspector Burdock, a closet music-lover, recognised the tune. He had heard it on the car radio only the other day. It seemed curiously at odds with Mrs Cresswell's taste in interior décor that she should listen to the *chaconne* from Bach's second partita.

The interview was even stickier than Burdock had anticipated. Oliver, it turned out, had neglected to tell his mother about the events of the previous day, and it took some minutes for the news to sink in. Mrs Cresswell's face gradually became a mottled shade of red under the discreet coating of powder, and finally she let out a genteel but piercing yell.

'Ollie! Ollie! Come here to Mummy this minute.'

The music stopped abruptly, and Oliver appeared holding a violin. At the sight of the two police officers, his face became closed and obstinate. He stood there silently under the barrage of questions and reproaches which followed, while Burdock cursed under his breath.

'I can't understand why no one bothered to let me know,' Mrs Cresswell wound up. 'I simply can't understand it. Who brought you home?'

Oliver unlocked his lips for long enough to say, 'Lin.'

Mrs Cresswell sighed heavily. 'Well, I suppose that accounts for it then. Though you really should have told Mummy, you know, darling.' She turned to Inspector Burdock, suddenly winsome and confidential. 'Lin Jensen, Inspector. She's a neighbour of ours, a painter. Quite well-known, as a matter of fact, though her pictures are a bit too *modern* for me, if you know what I mean. She's deaf and dumb, so it's understandable she didn't let me know.'

Oliver said sharply, 'She's bilingual, actually.'

'There's no need to be rude, Ollie darling.' She resumed her social smile. 'Ollie's been learning the deaf and dumb alphabet, you know.'

157

Mary Blossom decided to leave Inspector Burdock with the short straw. Mrs Cresswell displayed few signs of needing a woman's touch, indeed rather the reverse. She said, 'Would you like to show me the garden, Oliver. I think the inspector wants to have a quiet word with your mum.'

Oliver stomped crossly down the garden path, pulling leaves off plants. After a bit he burst out, 'She's the one that's dumb. *And* deaf. Why should I tell her things? She never listens.'

'And I expect you were feeling a bit upset, too. Sometimes when people are upset they don't want to talk about it. But you see we need you to help us find the murderer. Will you do that for us, Oliver?'

Oliver muttered ungraciously, 'I might. Depends what you want.'

'We want you to have a look at some photographs and see if you recognise anyone. And we thought you might like to have a talk with someone who could help you to remember things. You see, you may know more than you think you do, and in a murder investigation every detail counts.'

Oliver thought about it, slowly shredding his handful of leaves. 'All right,' he said eventually. 'I'll do it. But only if my mother isn't there.'

CHAPTER NINETEEN

Morgan, meanwhile, was driving slowly along the coast road. She still retained, from the much too bracing holidays which had punctuated her London childhood, the idea that sea air clears the brain. This evening, hers seemed paralysed, completely inert. She envied Ollie his fierce certainty that he knew where to pin the blame for Elspeth's death, his ability to make it part of a passionately constructed story. To Morgan, it seemed impossible to make either intellectual or emotional sense of a world from which Elspeth's sturdy presence had been so casually blotted out. Even the landscape through which she drove, the thickening dusk, the phosphorescent whiteness of the breaking waves, the grind and swirl of shingle sucked back in the undertow, seemed to symbolise only a bleak and desolate absence of meaning.

She had driven quite a long way before it occurred to her that this idea was a literary cliché, prompted by the 'melancholy, long, withdrawing roar' of the retreating tide in Matthew Arnold's *Dover Beach*. It was an occupational hazard of her profession that your most personal feelings and thoughts all too often turned out to be echoes of someone else's. Reflecting on how much she disliked Arnold and his smug Victorian gloom cheered her up a little, enough to make her decide to head for home. She still had the nagging sense that there was something she had seen but not recognised, some small but significant detail which might be the key to the cryptic letters Burdock had shown her, but she already knew that no amount of sea air was going to help her to retrieve it.

She swung the car round and headed back the way she had come, driving fast now through the gathering darkness. By the time she reached Hangman's Wood, it was already night. Her headlights cast a pallid glare over thick banks of roadside weeds. Trees were a looming blackness overhead. Somewhere in the tangled depths of the wood was the glade where Alka-Seltzer's dressed-up corpse had lolled grotesquely on Ben Gilbert's sky-blue blanket. Kidnapped from Elspeth's flat by two men in a blue BMW, Ollie had said. Morgan still couldn't see why anyone would want to kidnap and kill an old tomcat, but however he had come by his death, the manner of it made it a sinister precursor to Elspeth's own. Supposing Ollie was right, the catnappers must have stopped the car somewhere on this very road and flung the dead cat into the undergrowth where it had later been discovered by the kids who had put it in the pram.

Was Ben Gilbert too lying somewhere with a broken neck, a small decaying corpse hidden away among the trees? The police had searched the wood, but surely such a place had a thousand holes and burrows where a doll-sized bundle could be stowed, safe from the prying eyes of human searchers and the keen noses of dogs and scavenging foxes. Morgan shuddered and drove on, wanting lights and a warm house and the safe proximity of Lin. She knew with her adult self that there was no such thing as safety, but she found she was clutching at the thought of Lin as a terrified child clutches a stuffed toy. Love was a frail and delusive shelter from the darkness, but it was all she had.

The cottage, when she reached it, was like a beacon, with all the ground-floor windows lit up and golden. As she walked up the garden path, she could see Lin standing at the kitchen table calmly chopping vegetables. The fear which had taken possession of her in Hangman's Wood still ran coldly through Morgan's veins and made the open curtains seem like an invitation to the lurking terrors of the night to press invisible faces against the windowpanes. More rationally, with a killer on the loose it seemed reckless of Lin to advertise the fact that she was alone in a remote cottage. Morgan went inside and twitched the curtains shut, feeling annoyed with herself at this betrayal of female pride and self-reliance. Lin looked up and smiled then bent her head over the onion she was carefully reducing to wafer-thin translucent rings.

Morgan went over to bury her face in the soft cascade of Lin's pale hair. The scent of herbal shampoo and the perfume of warm skin mingled with the sharp smell of onions. Stinging onion tears began to well up in Morgan's eyes. Lin kept on slicing, dry-eyed and impervious. Morgan walked round to the other side of the table. Her hands said, 'Leave that. Come and sit on the sofa with me.'

Lin, her hands too busy to sign, smiled at her briefly and said, 'Soon.' She went over to the stove and scooped the onion rings into a large casserole. There was a sizzle of oil and the different and friendlier smell of onions starting to cook. Lin returned to the table to section a green and a red pepper with Japanese precision. Morgan, defeated, wandered over to the dresser to find the gin bottle.

To all appearances, this was the normal, placid pattern of everyday life; Lin cooking, Morgan pouring them both a drink, then supper, watching television together perhaps, desultory chat about how they had spent the day, bed. In fact, Morgan knew that both of them were putting off the moment of talking about what she had done that afternoon. Eventually she would tell Lin about her visit to the mortuary but not yet, not this evening. Elspeth had been her friend rather than Lin's, had belonged, in fact, to a side of her life that Lin was reluctant to share, and yet Lin, more than anyone, would have understood the sculptural power of that still, cold face on the mortuary slab. Perhaps, as an artist, she could have looked at it calmly and without anguish. Morgan realised how badly she needed to free herself from that deathly coldness in Lin's living embrace. She went over to the table and took her by the hand. Lin came, unresisting.

In the sitting-room Morgan closed the curtains, turned off the lights, drew Lin down onto the sofa. Death, she remembered, was supposed to be a great aphrodisiac. Now, as the impersonal ferocity of lovemaking began to obliterate all other thoughts, all other needs, she understood why. She felt no more tenderness than if Lin had been some chance-met stranger, all that mattered was that she was alive, alive. There was only this present moment, these urgent caresses, the warm contact of skin on skin. Touch was a healing magic; Morgan was hungry for it and the temporary forgetfulness it brought.

After a while Lin slid out of her arms and went to rescue the onions before they browned to a crisp. Morgan sighed and let herself return to reality. She looked at her watch and realised that she ought to turn on the news. It would be sensible to see how Elspeth's death was being reported. The university term was about to start and parents up and down the country must be panicking at the idea of their sons and daughters (especially their daughters, Morgan thought wryly) returning to a campus stalked by a mystery killer. The anxious phone calls must already have begun and so must whatever defensive line the university had managed to cobble together.

It was strange how being involved in a local disaster bleached the horror out of global ones that would otherwise have concerned her. News items about African famine, floods in Bangladesh, Russian aggression were simply postponements of what she wanted to hear. Lin came back and sat beside her, fiddling with the remote control to access the subtitles. A compulsive reader of any print that fell under her eye, Morgan began to follow them. The impersonal voice of the newscaster sounded like an inane echo.

'The elderly woman whose body was discovered yesterday in a residence block at Oxbourne University has been named as Dr Elspeth Blair-Guthrie. Police are treating her death as murder. Dr Blair-Guthrie, a well-known anthropologist, narrowly escaped death once before in South America ...'

A black and white picture of a much younger Elspeth surrounded by naked tribesmen illustrated the brief summary of her life. With one of those queasy swoops into flippancy that tended to afflict her at funerals, Morgan found herself wondering if it was politically incorrect to use the term tribesmen even when the tribespersons in question were all conspicuously male. Probably. And there was something else about the picture, something she couldn't quite put her finger on. In any case, it had already been replaced by tomorrow's weather forecast. Morgan took the remote control from Lin and switched off.

They spent a peaceful evening together. Lin dished up ratatouille, Morgan opened a bottle of wine, they talked about ordinary, domestic things as they shared the washing-up. They both felt the need to reassert the security of the bond between them, to shut out the surrounding darkness. They went to bed early and made love again, gently and tenderly. They slept. Hours later, Morgan woke as abruptly as if a voice had spoken in her ear. Careful not to wake Lin, she slid out of bed and went downstairs to hunt for a Bible and a biblical concordance. The references she needed were easy to find. After a while she phoned the police station.

'This is Dr Morgan Byrd speaking. I'd like to leave a message for Inspector Burdock. Tell him I think I may have cracked his code.'

CHAPTER TWENTY

One way and another, by Tuesday morning Burdock was feeling slightly more optimistic about the case. He called in Crewe and Mary Blossom for a brisk briefing session.

'All right, here's the state of play. We still haven't managed to get hold of the next of kin. Apparently, he's somewhere in the wilds of Turkey on an all-party fact-finding commission into the plight of the Kurds, but his secretary is trying to get a message through to him.

'The lab people have finished with that photograph of the Cresswell boy. The thumbprint is blood all right, but not human. Seems it was a chicken, and not a frozen one out of Sainsbury's either.'

'Black mass, sir,' said Crewe brightly. 'Don't they sacrifice a cock? Sounds as if we might be looking at a whole paedophile ring.' The cheerfulness went out of his face as a further thought struck him. 'If you can believe all you read in the papers, they sacrifice babies too.'

'Though no one has ever come up with a cast-iron case,' added Mary Blossom sturdily.

'Anyway, if McBride is part of whatever's going on, he hasn't left his dabs,' said Burdock. 'The thing was covered in prints, but none belonging to anyone we know apart from the deceased. Apparently, there's something distinctive about the shape of the thumbprint, but that doesn't get us anywhere.

'That mugshot of McBride has arrived from Glasgow. Crewe, I want you to show it to anyone who was around on the day of the kidnapping, starting with the next-door neighbour and the sister-in-law. Oh, and see if you can get them to be a bit more specific about times. I want to know how much leeway Melanie Wilson would have had. And I suppose we ought to interview Melanie again while we're at it, not that it'll do any good. Sergeant, if you could just nip up to the hospital and see what you can do.'

Here we go again, thought Mary Blossom. The old women-and-children routine. Might as well be a lifeboat on the Titanic. As demurely as she could, she said. 'I do have a name, sir.'

Burdock looked sheepish, as she had intended him to. 'I can't go round calling you Blossom, Sergeant. People might get hold of the wrong idea.'

'Call me Cherry, sir. Everyone else does. What line do you

want me to take with Melanie, supposing I can get her to utter at all?'

'As I see it, there are two main possibilities. Most likely the kidnapping was arranged by Craik and his chums and Melanie was coaxed into going along with it. On the other hand, we know that McBride is a pervert and a sadist. Melanie's evidence sent him down for seven years. Maybe he figured the best way to get back at her was to take Ben and then let her know what he'd done to him.'

'And that could account for why she feels responsible. On the other hand, all that guilt stuff may be to do with the abortion. Didn't Dr Byrd say she talked as if the dead baby was a girl?'

'See what you can do anyway, Sergeant ... ah, hmm, Cherry.'

'Wilco, sir.'

She grinned at Burdock, who said stodgily, 'I shall be checking out how uniforms are getting on up at the campus. Oh, and Dr Byrd seems to have come up with something on those letters. You were right about that one, Crewe. Though I don't expect it's significant. Seems that besides the savages Dr Blair-Guthrie had a sideline in funny sects. Our holy chum was probably just part of her research material.'

Not surprisingly, the interview with Melanie got nowhere. She sat listless and mute until Mary Blossom worked round to the subject of McBride, at which point she went a bluish white and started rocking and whimpering until a fiercely protective nurse showed Mary the door. Crewe had rather better luck. The next-door neighbour shook her head regretfully over the photograph, plainly wishing she could have enhanced her own role in the drama by recognising the villain. Otherwise, she told exactly the same story as before. She really couldn't swear to the exact time she had taken her washing in, but she was positive that she had seen Ben himself and not just the pram. She definitely remembered Melanie lifting him out and hugging him and making sure his nappy was dry before tucking him back in again. Really fond of the kiddy, she had seemed. Proper shame it was, wasn't it. Those poor, poor parents. It kept her awake at night sometimes wondering where the poor little mite had got to.

Rosalind Gilbert, on the other hand, proved unexpectedly helpful. She struck Crewe as a twitchy kind of woman, though with a nephew kidnapped and a close acquaintance murdered that was understandable enough. As she talked, she held an overdressed infant on her knee, nervously smoothing down flounces and straightening a lacy mob cap. She hesitated over the picture of McBride, biting her lip indecisively, but eventually said that no, she didn't think she recognised him. Nor could she remember exactly what time she had walked past her sister-in-law's house. Round about tea-time was the best she could manage. However, she was quite certain she knew who was responsible not only for the kidnapping but also for the murder.

'It's one of those animal rights groups. It has to be. My husband has had death threats you know, really horrible text messages and letters.'

Crewe did his best not to sound too sceptical. 'And you think this animal rights group might have had reason to kill Dr Blair-Guthrie?'

Mrs Gilbert stared at him. 'Well of course they did. It was poor Elspeth who was really responsible for that drug that Andrew's been working on. It began with a paper they wrote together five years ago on the pharmacopoeia of the rain forest. There was a television programme about it on the very day those monsters took poor little Benjie. It all fits in.'

'Ah, right. Yes. That's very interesting,' said Crewe, wondering what a pharmacopoeia might be. 'These death threats, now. Can you put a date on them?'

'A few months ago. I can't remember exactly. Andrew reported them to the police at the time but of course nothing was done about it.'

'I suppose you don't still have the messages themselves?'

'I don't really know what Andrew did with them. He probably just deleted the texts and tore up the letters. He's abroad at the moment so you see it's all a bit ...' She broke off and bent her head over the child, murmuring, 'Daddy's gone away, hasn't he, Zeffie darling? But the details will all be in your records, surely?' she added waspishly, turning her attention back to Crewe. 'You do keep records of that sort of thing, I suppose?'

'Oh we do, yes,' said Crewe, suddenly wrong-footed. She had seemed such a mild, soft-spoken little woman.

Her voice rose shrilly. 'Then why don't you do something about it before we're all murdered in our beds?' She gasped and broke off, then said apologetically, 'I'm so sorry. It's the strain, you see, being alone in the house with Andrew not here and worrying all the time in case anything happens to Zeffie.'

'I quite understand,' said Crewe sympathetically. 'We really are doing our level best to catch the bastard, if you'll pardon the expression. You've been a tremendous help, Mrs Gilbert. I'll see to it that the business of the death threats is followed up right away.'

Andrew Gilbert had indeed reported a couple of unpleasant anonymous letters the previous autumn, probably provoked by a newspaper article about his work. They had been considerably more inventive than the laconic message purporting to come from Ben Gilbert's kidnapper and had been posted in London. The television programme proved even easier to check out. PC Taylor had recorded it for his daughter, who was hoping to go to medical school next year.

Crewe's pleasure at announcing a new and promising

link between the two crimes was somewhat dampened by the discovery that the inspector had already received much the same information from Dr Byrd. It had proved to be the one small breakthrough in Burdock's day. The intense police activity on campus had so far achieved very little apart from creating a mixture of alarm and reassurance in the breasts of anxious Volvo-driving parents delivering their student offspring for the start of term. Dr Blair-Guthrie's attacker seemed to have left a clean slate behind him. It wasn't difficult to see how he might have got into the flat. The windows of the staff accommodation block had catches which could be eased open with a knife blade and the victim had lived on the ground floor. However, he had left no prints or other traces and nothing obvious had been stolen, though it was impossible to tell if papers or valuables had been removed from the ransacked study. Of course, even lack of evidence is evidence of a kind. The manner of the killing, with no weapon and no blood, suggested either a real professional, possibly trained in unarmed combat, or an opportunistic assailant with hideous beginner's luck who had probably fled terrified and empty-handed at the realisation of what he had done. Well, if it was the latter, they would get him sooner or later. He would panic and give himself away.

Burdock had also had an exasperating session with the Bursar, giving advice about basic security measures which should have been incorporated years ago. There seemed to be hardly a building in the entire university that could not have been broken into in ten seconds flat by a delinquent child armed with a stick of liquorice. Among the few exceptions were the animal houses, which had been provided with window grills and sophisticated alarm systems after the trouble the previous term. Burdock interviewed the head technician, a glum middle-aged man with a weary philosophical manner, who was able to give him the names of some at least of the students who had taken part in the demonstration.

'They don't mean any real harm, you know, students. They just get carried away. You have to remember that a lot of them see this place as a sort of glorified Wendy house where they can play at politics without having to get real. It never occurs to them that they're fouling up someone else's workplace. The Craik boy, though, he was something different. There was a nasty streak of violence there.'

Dr Byrd had been equally discouraging about his chances of unearthing an animal liberationist cell.

'You'll probably find they're all nice middle-class kids who had pet rabbits when they were little,' she predicted cynically. 'Be prepared to listen to a lot of heart-rending stuff about baby seals and kittens with shampoo in their eyes. Don't get me wrong. I'm not too sure about the ethics of animal testing myself. But when I was a student we marched against the war in Iraq.'

'Yes, and what about the waste of police time that your lot caused?' said Burdock, suddenly waspish.

For an instant she glared at him with all the force of that ancient antagonism, then she laughed. 'Young people ought to be angry about injustice, Inspector. It worries me that my own students aren't angry enough. If Lawrence Craik really has terrorist cronies, I don't think you'll find them here.'

This seemed discouragingly likely. However, what Dr Byrd had to tell him about the anonymous letters seemed to Burdock to put Lawrence Craik even more firmly in the centre of the picture.

'It suddenly occurred to me last night that there is a name that the writer is obsessed with but never mentions. The letters keep coming back to the story of Ishmael. That isn't so surprising in itself, of course. Ishmael has become established in the popular imagination as the symbol of the outcast and the loner. Think of *Moby Dick*, for example.'

Burdock thought and was puzzled. Rattling good yarn about whaling, wasn't it? Sort of thing Craik and his friends wanted to put a stop to. Well, he could see their point about that, but laboratory rats, now... Burdock blinked and forced himself to concentrate. Dr Byrd's expository tone had taken him back to English lessons at school and provoked the same response, a dozy lack of attention at the back of the class. The point of her lecture appeared to be that the letter-writer was identifying not himself, as a putative loner and outcast, but some third party with this Ishmael character, whoever he might be.

Dr Byrd read the bafflement on his face and came to his rescue. 'Abraham's wife Sarah can't have children so she tells him to sleep with her Egyptian handmaid and he does and fathers Ishmael. But Hagar, the maid, starts gloating about being the one with the kid, so Sarah throws her out. It's all in Genesis.'

Burdock was shocked. 'They never told us that in Sunday school. I thought Abraham was supposed to be a saint.'

'A patriarch, Inspector. It's not the same thing. Anyway, Hagar wanders in the wilderness until all their water is used up, then she lays the child under a bush and sits apart from him and weeps.'

Burdock knew the next bit. 'And she says let me not see the death of the child?'

'Correct. But God opens her eyes and shows her a well of water, so they both survive after all.'

'So where does that get us?'

'Possibly nowhere. But last night I was watching the news and they showed a photograph of Elspeth in the Amazon jungle and I had a feeling I'd seen it before. And then I remembered a programme a few weeks ago about the Gilbert brothers' research and Elspeth's connection with it.'

'Connection?'

'Yes, it was her rain forest Indians who discovered the vital ingredient of this new drug they've developed. Anyhow, there was a sequence about the baby that James has been testing the drug on and I'm sure it was called Ishmael. I remember thinking poor little bugger, imagine saddling a kid with a name like that. It could be just a coincidence, of course.'

Burdock thought it probably was. The whole story seemed too fancy to be plausible, what with Egyptian handmaids and adulterous patriarchs. He was far more interested in the discovery of a link between Dr Blair-Guthrie and James Gilbert. After Crewe and Mary Blossom had reported on the day's progress and gone off to the canteen, he sat turning it over in his mind. Suppose one of Craik's animal lib friends had decided to have a snoop round the victim's flat, or even to confront her about her part in the Gilberts' experiments. Dr Byrd had said she was a brave and outspoken woman. Could there have been an argument that got out of hand and turned to violence?

There was a knock at the door and Crewe came back into the office grinning from ear to ear. 'Present for you, sir,' he said jauntily. 'Simpson and Hale have found a suspicious character wandering round the campus so they've brought him in for questioning. They reckon he must be our religious maniac .'

CHAPTER TWENTY-ONE

It was Collington who had raised the alarm. A panic button had been fitted in the porter's lodge only that morning, and when a wild-eyed, bearded tramp had wandered in and started a rambling monologue in which the name of Elspeth Blair-Guthrie had featured along with the destruction of the wicked and the punishment of the workers of iniquity, Collington had pressed it. By the time Burdock came down to the interview room, the suspect was refusing to say anything at all.

'He won't give his name and we couldn't get him to sign for his possessions. But he was carrying this.' Simpson proffered a well-worn Bible with an inscription on the flyleaf: 'For our dear son Enoch. May he be sealed among the servants of God.'

'That was all he had on him except for a hankie and a little loose change. Oh, and a sort of amulet affair. Kind of lucky charm. He didn't want to part with that, or with the Bible either. We offered him a Gideon one in exchange but he didn't seem keen.'

The man sitting stock still and bolt upright in the interview room looked rather like Burdock's hazy idea of a patriarch, but one who had fallen on hard times. He had a flowing grey beard of biblical proportions, matted and tangled with leaves and bits of dried grass. His face, above this dishevelled cascade of hair, was hollow-cheeked and ashen and the rims of his eyes looked red and sore. He wore a heavy black suit, oddly cut and old-fashioned, a coarse linen shirt like something out of a museum, and a kind of black cravat twisted round his neck. His clothes had been neatly darned and patched in places, but were crumpled and grubby as if he had recently been sleeping rough. His hands, laid flat on the table in front of him, looked to Burdock more like a workman's hands than a tramp's. The despised Gideon Bible lay where he had pushed it aside, along with a wide-brimmed black felt hat. When Burdock spoke to him, he simply stared with those painful eyes and said nothing.

Burdock switched on the recorder, cleared his throat and spoke the preliminaries into it. This usually produced a visible reaction in even the most recalcitrant prisoner but the man in black continued to sit like a waxwork. Burdock wondered whether he could possibly be deaf. He leaned forward across the table, fixed his suspect or witness with an answering stare and said loudly and clearly, 'I am Detective Chief Inspector Burdock. I am investigating the murder of Dr Elspeth Blair-Guthrie and I have reason to believe you may be able to assist the police with their inquiries. To start with, I need to know your name.'

The man in black stirred fractionally from his inflexible pose. 'So Elspeth Blair-Guthrie has been taken? I had not heard.' His hoarse voice was not exactly foreign but somehow distinctive. It was also oddly lacking in inflections, so that it was impossible for Burdock to guess whether he felt surprise or regret or even whether he was lying. He could tell, though, that the man's throat was very dry. He switched off the recorder and told Simpson to fetch some tea. This provoked a harsh, almost violent, gesture of rejection. Burdock shrugged and switched on the recorder again. He said, 'Just tell me your name, would you.'

No answer, only that burning stare.

'Are you called Enoch?'

Again no answer.

'You knew Dr Blair-Guthrie, I take it?'

'She was a stranger to me.'

'Then why were you asking for her this afternoon?'

This time the silence was accompanied by an expressionless shake of the head. Burdock tried all the variations of menace and reassurance he could muster but got no further. He had the impression that his interviewee was both frightened and distressed, but his obstinate muteness did not seem to be caused by mental confusion. Rather, he gave the sense of a strong and vigorous personality which had somehow lost its bearings, though perhaps this was an illusion created by the striking eyes and the beard. Finally he gave up trying and Simpson led the man away.

'What do you reckon,' he asked Crewe. 'Is he just a harmless loony or does he know something?'

'He knows something all right, sir. I'm sure he does.'

'But like practically everyone else in this bloody case, he's not letting on what it is. Ah well, it'll do no harm to let him sweat for a bit. We've got enough evidence to hold him. Sounds as if he was spouting some pretty incriminating stuff when Simpson and Hale first appeared on the scene.'

'Do you think he did it, sir? Murdered the old lady.'

Burdock always told himself he didn't believe in hunches. He certainly didn't believe in airing them to subordinate officers. He shook his head with ponderous professional tact. 'Too early to say, Crewe. Much too early to say.'

CHAPTER TWENTY-TWO

Oliver had hoped that the photographs he was to look at would be of the men in the blue BMW, though he had only caught a hurried glimpse of them through the car window and was not at all sure that he could recognise them again. He was quite certain, though, that all the men in the pictures Inspector Burdock and Sergeant Blossom showed him were complete strangers. None of them had black hair for a start and though one had a moustache, it was the wrong shape.

The final photograph turned out to be a trap. Inspector Burdock slid it in front of him and said, 'Do you recognise this, lad? We found it among Dr Blair-Guthrie's things.'

For a moment Oliver was completely taken aback, then he remembered Cathy and Stephanie and their lies about playing at dollies. 'Oh, that,' he said indifferently. 'That was just a game.'

Sergeant Blossom leaned forward intently. 'What sort of a game? Who did you play it with, Ollie?'

Oliver shrugged. 'Oh, you know. Just people.'

'Grown-up people?'

Oliver let his voice fill with ten-year-old scorn. 'You think grown-ups play at being rain forest Indians? Fat chance.'

The inspector eyed him hard, so that it was an effort to prevent himself from wriggling. 'Older boys, was it, then, sonny? Just let me have their names, would you?'

'No I won't. Why on earth should I? We haven't done anything wrong.' The indignation was real even if the innocence was faked.

The inspector sighed. 'You have to be reasonable, lad. I'm investigating a murder here, and someone put that picture in the victim's flat.'

Oliver opened his eyes wide, achieving what he hoped was a look of perfect candour. 'Oh, I did that. I took it with me. I wanted to look something up.'

Burdock sighed again, more heavily. 'You're telling me that you and these mystery chums of yours were pretending to be savages and you took this photograph to the deceased woman's flat because you wanted to check you'd got all the details right.' His voice had a sceptical ring to it. Oliver nodded, cautious and mute.

Sergeant Blossom said firmly, 'It doesn't sound a very nice game, Ollie, letting them take your picture in the altogether and then mutilate it like that.'

'It's called scarifying, actually. Elspeth told me that in cultures where people don't wear many clothes they often decorate their bodies instead.'

These scholarly details were lost on Sergeant Blossom. 'You really ought to tell us who else was involved, you know.'

'I'd rather not, thanks.'

'I take it it was just the photo that got sliced? No one's taken a razor blade to you personally?'

'Course not. See for yourself.' Oliver peeled off his sweater and turned round to show bony shoulder blades protruding, unharmed, from his clean white vest. They let him go home then, but the feeling of lucky escape was less strong than his disappointment at failing to spot the two assassins. He had a second murder to avenge now, and so far the grown-ups had been no help at all.

His sessions with Dr White, the child psychologist, were just as useless, though they were interesting in a way. They took place in an odd room full of big floppy dolls. Oliver had not really meant to tell her anything; he was still waiting for a reply to his letter to Torquil Guthrie and he had every intention of keeping his mouth shut until it came. However, Dr White turned out to be someone it was difficult not to talk to. It was not that she was at all friendly or sympathetic. In fact she was so neutral that she hardly seemed to be there at all. Even her name might have been chosen to suggest a blank sheet of paper. Conversations with her were like some peculiar board game in which it was always his move. It took Oliver several sessions to work out what the rules were.

The first time he saw her, she began by asking how he felt about his family.

'My mother's all right, I suppose. Well, she's a little bit stupid, actually. I don't have a father.'

'How do you feel about your parents separating?'

'They didn't. I never had a father to begin with. Mum got me from a sperm bank, a special one in America for people who want really brainy kids. Mum says my donor probably had a Nobel Prize.'

'And how do you feel about that, Oliver?'

'Oh, she only thinks it because I'm good at maths. I asked Dr Blair-Guthrie about it once and she said it was more likely to have been someone who was learning to be a doctor. She told me about these three girls who lived in Poland or somewhere and their father wanted to make them really good at chess. He wasn't much good at it himself, he just chose chess because girls were supposed to be hopeless at it. Anyway, he never let them do anything else and they all became world famous. I've never done much except maths, so you'd expect me to be pretty good at it really.'

'I see. And how do you feel about not having a father, Oliver?'

'How do you mean? I wouldn't want a father who made me play chess all day.'

'I mean, would you have preferred it if your mother had had you in some other way?'

'Not really. Well she couldn't have, could she? We did all about it at school last term, the sperm and the egg. It's called human reproduction and if it's a different sperm then someone else gets born instead of you. There are billions of them, so you have to be pretty lucky just to be here at all.'

Dr White sighed and tried again. Oliver registered that he had somehow scored a point in the game. 'How do you feel about your mother not having a husband?'

'Oh, she did. He was quite a lot older than her and they didn't have any children and then he died. I'm called after him, actually. He was a banker. He had loads of investments and stuff. That's how Mum could afford to have me.'

'And do you have any uncles, Oliver?'

'No, Mum was an only like me.'

'Ah yes. Well, does your mother have any close men friends?'

'She has some friends she plays bridge with.'

'I see. Well now, Oliver, would you like to do me a painting of how you feel about an important male person in your life?'

There was a small table already set out for painting, with a big pad of sugar paper and some jars of poster paint. 'All right,' said Oliver, 'but I don't like people looking over my shoulder.'

He painted in a rather half-hearted way. It seemed a silly thing to be doing, with Elspeth dead and the murderer not caught. There wasn't anything to mix the paint in, so he had to try to mix it on the paper, which was all rough and lumpy. The brush was scratchy too, like an old toothbrush, not like the sleek ones that Lin let him use. After a bit he gave up and said, 'OK, I've finished.'

He could sense that Dr White didn't like his painting much but she asked him to tell her about it all the same.

'That's Alka-Seltzer, my cat. Well, I sort of had part shares in him. Actually he's dead now. I did a better painting of him once, but this brush is pretty rotten.'

Dr White sighed again and looked at her watch and said she would see him tomorrow.

The following day Oliver tried to change the rules of the game by talking about the men in the blue BMW. Dr White asked him a lot of pointless questions about them that didn't seem to lead anywhere and finally asked him to do a painting of them.

'I'll do a drawing if you'll lend me a biro. And let me have a proper piece of paper.'

This time he really concentrated, but he had never been any good at drawing people and the harder he thought about what the men had looked like, the vaguer his memories of them seemed to become. There were only two details he was sure about, so he wrote 'BLACK HAIR' under one portrait and 'MUSTASH' under the other. He did a separate drawing of the car, making quite a good job of it, then added a back view to show the number plate.

'Could you give this to Inspector Burdock, please? It's very important.'

'Why is that, Oliver?'

'Just he might find it useful in his investigation.'

'Very well then. I'll see you again tomorrow.'

Rather drearily, Oliver wondered what for. Dr White wasn't helping him to remember things at all, and anyway his university term had started. It didn't seem to be part of the game to say so, but he had already decided he was playing for a draw. He was pretty sure Dr White was beginning to feel as discouraged as he was.

In the third session, she started asking him questions about Elspeth. This was dangerous ground and Oliver's answers became short and cagey. After a bit, and rather to his surprise, she mentioned the men in the blue BMW. Yesterday she hadn't seemed to be all that interested in them.

'Those men you told me about yesterday, have they hurt you in some way, Oliver? Would you like to paint me a picture of how you feel about that?'

Suddenly Oliver realised what the rough paper and the rough brush were for. They were for making huge angry paintings of grief and rage and loss, thick red and black and yellow daubs of violence and revenge. He worked in a controlled frenzy, forgetting who and where he was, the tears he would never have shown to anyone running unnoticed down his cheeks. He wiped his nose on the back of his hand like a little kid and snot got onto the painting and paint got onto his face as he struggled to express the black and bloody emptiness inside him.

Finishing the painting was like waking up with a heavy cold, exhausted and groggy and with his nose bunged up, to find Dr White at his elbow with a box of tissues asking him to explain what he had done.

'That's Alka-Seltzer my cat and that's Elspeth. They're lying on the ground like that because they're dead.'

'And how about this figure at the top?'

'That's me.'

'And what are you holding, Oliver?' He had painted himself naked, with a Kainu hunting spear in his hand, standing huge and powerful above the murdered bodies, menacing their killers.

'It's a spear.'

Dr White spoke in a special voice as if she knew the game had reached a crucial stage and she was winning. 'Did the men in the blue BMW ask you to show them your spear, Oliver?

Did they show you theirs, perhaps? Is that why you feel so upset?'

Oliver stared at her blankly and then suddenly he realised what she was talking about. He went very red. This woman was just like Cathy and Stephanie with their furtive, nudging innuendoes. With all the dignity he could muster he said, 'Actually, I think you must be a very stupid person.'

In exactly the same tone as before, Dr White asked, 'Why do you think that, Oliver?'

Oliver found that he was shouting at the top of his voice. 'Because you're a horrible, horrible cow and you don't understand anything. Elspeth was my friend. She was my friend and somebody murdered her. They broke her neck and they broke Alka-Seltzer's neck and I hate them, I hate them, I'd like to kill them and I'm going to kill them, that's why I'm holding a spear.'

Dr White still wore her neutral expression, as if her face had been programmed to look equally detached whatever anyone said to her. Oliver broke off and stared at her, panting. He took a deep breath and found that his throat hurt.

He said flatly, 'I'm going home now,' and walked out of the room before she could ask him again how he felt.

CHAPTER TWENTY-THREE

Dr Byrd had been right about the animal liberation students. Inspector Burdock spent a fruitless afternoon interviewing a succession of Matthews, Sophies and Charlottes. Some of them launched into long and articulate defences of their ideological position. Some of them gave him leaflets about factory farming and the fur trade. They were well-meaning, idealistic and sincere and they burned with a shared conviction that right feeling and reasoned argument had the power to change the world. None of them seemed capable of hurting a fly or indeed, Burdock reflected wryly, running a whelk stall, let alone organising a successful kidnap. They were plainly shocked by the way the animal house demo had got out of hand and bitter about Lawrence Craik's betrayal of their creed of non-violence, but if he had any links to more sinister idealists they appeared to be genuinely unaware of it.

The child psychologist had drawn a blank with young Oliver, too. She reported that though there were some indications of identity confusion and emotional disturbance, she had not been able to find any clear signs of sexual abuse. Before she left, she punctiliously handed over a folded piece of paper.

'Oliver asked me to give you this. He seemed to feel it was important '

Burdock unfolded it and chuckled. 'Mugshots of the villains, eh? And an artist's impression of the get-away car. Very thoughtful of him. It's as good a lead as anything else I've got at the moment, I'll give him that.' Relishing the joke, he pinned the drawing to his noticeboard.

When she heard about Dr White's conclusions, Sergeant Blossom was considerably less amused.

'Something kinky's going on, sir. I'm sure of it. That story he cooked up for us sounded like a pack of lies to me from start to finish.'

Thrust back onto the horns of a dilemma, Burdock lost his temper. 'OK, so he's lying. What do you expect me to do about it? Interrogate him until he cracks? Start a bloody great witch-hunt and have him end up in care?'

Mary Blossom stuck to her guns. 'I'm concerned about him, sir. He's only a kid.'

'He's a neurotic, self-advertising little time-waster with a nasty line in make-believe,' Burdock said savagely. 'I bet you anything you like, if we followed this business up, we would find he had initiated the whole thing.'

'So that's all right then, is it, sir?'

Seeing her face, Burdock modified his tone. 'Look, I understand your concern, Cherry, but we've done all we sensibly can. We've had him checked over for obvious damage and, more to the point, we've alerted his Mum to the problem. He'll be lucky if he isn't still under house arrest when he makes the Guinness Book of Records as Britain's youngest ever professor.'

'I suppose so.'

'And what's more, twenty to one it has nothing to do with the case. He told us he put that photograph in Dr Blair-Guthrie's flat himself and I'm prepared to believe him unless and until I have evidence to the contrary. I'm keeping an open mind on it, but that isn't the same thing as leaping to conclusions and causing no end of trouble in the process.'

Evidence, of whatever kind, seemed conspicuous by its absence. With neither of his two main avenues of inquiry yielding any results, Burdock decided to follow up Dr Byrd's suggestion about the significance of the religious letters. Despite further questioning, they had got nowhere with the inscrutable Enoch and Burdock had begun to wonder uneasily whether he was really only holding him as a mascot. Being able to say that a man was helping the police with their inquiries had usefully kept the press and the Super off his back for a bit, but subsequent interviews had only reinforced his original conviction that, whatever human interest story might account for his moody silence, Enoch was simply a distraction and a waste of valuable time. Sorting out the identity of James Gilbert's small patient should tidy him out of the picture.

A stony-faced Sister Maxwell showed him into the surgeon's office. Burdock understood that she blamed him equally whether he was bringing bad news or the no news that was almost worse for Ben's stricken parents. In the weeks since his son's disappearance, James Gilbert had changed beyond recognition. Though he was as neatly dressed and meticulously shaved as ever, the haunted look on his face reminded Burdock vividly of the mute and wretched tramp whose intransigence had brought him here. His skin had a greyish tinge and his eyes had retreated into their sockets as if from many nights of watching. It seemed to be only the carapace of his professional manner that was holding him together as he courteously answered Burdock's questions.

'I think you must mean Isaac Potter, Inspector. His mother calls him Ishmael. He has Beaufort-Lindgren's disease, a congenital malfunction of the liver combined with other complications which lead to a gradual breakdown of the immune system. The background to the case is rather interesting, as a matter of fact. Beaufort-Lindgren's is quite rare in the general population, perhaps one in a hundred and twenty thousand births, but the Potter child belongs to the Sealed Brethren, a small inbred religious community in which the incidence is more like one in twenty-five. Two of the mother's younger siblings died of the disease so she spotted the signs early, sooner than many GPs would have done. The Brethren don't believe in medical interventions, and in fact up until now there has been no effective treatment for the condition, which is usually fatal by the age of two. The clinical history of the community first came to my attention some years ago when Elspeth Blair-Guthrie did a pioneering anthropological study. They are a closed sect and don't readily talk to outsiders. It was she who managed to persuade Mrs Potter to bring Isaac to me. Mrs Potter is a widow, I believe, and as far as I know she had no one else to turn to. I really can't imagine that the case would cause anyone to want to harm either Ben or Dr Blair-Guthrie. Isaac is making excellent progress. Indeed, if you wanted to be dramatic about it, you could say I have probably saved his life.'

'That's very helpful, sir,' said Burdock. 'Now I'd like to have a few words with the mother, if I may.'

'Yes, certainly. Sister, would you ask Mrs Potter to come along to the office.'

Sister Maxwell shot Burdock a reproachful look and left the room, the clack of her heels conveying more clearly than words that he had now committed that sin against the holy ghost, 'disturbing one of my mothers.' The door swung shut behind her with nicely judged sharpness.

In the same impersonal tone as before, the voice of a doctor discussing a patient, James Gilbert said, 'At least if we knew what had happened to Ben, and were able to bury him, it might be easier for Libby to come to terms with it.'

Feeling and sounding like a poorly practised liar, Burdock repeated the usual empty litany of comfort. Most small babies were cared for rather than harmed by their abductors. Missing babies had been discovered alive and well after much longer periods. The police were making every effort to recover Ben. It was essential not to give up hope.

For the first time, James Gilbert's face showed a glimmer of human emotion. It appeared to be pure hatred. 'Hope is a dangerous drug, Inspector,' he said dryly. 'After repeated doses it can become a toxic one. Now, if you'll excuse me, I have patients to attend to.'

Burdock waited alone in the office, fidgeting unhappily, until Sister Maxwell came back shepherding a dowdy middle-aged woman. There was no doubt that Mrs Potter was acquainted with the mysterious Enoch. As soon as Burdock showed her the Bible and the amulet, she gasped and covered her face.

Sister Maxwell patted her shoulder and fixed Burdock with a basilisk glare. 'Now don't take on, dear,' she ordered firmly. 'I'm sure the inspector didn't mean to upset you.'

Behind the shielding hands it was evident that Mrs Potter was weeping. In a muffled voice she said, 'It's been my fault. All of it. It's all been my fault.'

Describing the scene to Sergeant Crewe later in the day, Burdock was slightly rueful about what had followed. 'Rightly speaking, you could say I got the whole tale out of her on false pretences, though I didn't realise that until after she'd spilled the beans. Apparently that lucky charm was something they set a lot of store by. Sort of a heavenly membership card as you might say. As soon as she saw it she jumped to conclusions and thought her husband must be dead. Assumed he wouldn't have given it up else.'

'So Enoch's her husband?'

'Well, strictly speaking he's her ex. He wouldn't agree to let the child go for treatment so she left him. The Brethren don't hold with modern medicine, think it's the devil's work, but she'd watched two of her brothers die of the same thing when she was a kid and she couldn't face it for her own child. She feels as guilty as hell about it, though. Thinks she's gone against the law of God. Seems she told her husband she'd been sleeping around and the child wasn't his so he threw the pair of them out. He must be a proper fool to believe her. She's a drab little sparrow of a woman with a face like a nun, pushing fifty if she's a day. And unworldly with it, though you'd expect that of course. I think it was almost more of a shock for her to find out her husband's in police custody than to imagine he'd snuffed it. She kept saying, "Enoch's a good man". Turned out she didn't even know the Gilbert baby was missing, though they'd told her about Dr Blair-Guthrie. Been brought up never to read the papers. She told me the Brethren have no truck with the vain conversation of Babylon. Amazing really in this day and age.'

'So Enoch Potter had a motive. He'd lost his own son and he blamed it on James Gilbert.'

'And Dr Blair-Guthrie had advised his wife to seek medical advice so he blamed her too. We don't need to worry about how the assailant got into the flat. She'd have opened the door to him. And then they had a confrontation and he killed her.'

'Though why would he search the study?'

'Christ knows. To make it look like a burglary perhaps, though I doubt he has the cunning to think of it. Anyway, that's a detail. The important thing is, could he have done it or does he have an alibi?'

'Only one way to find out, sir. Though I wouldn't get too excited. Religious communities tend to be pretty nosy places. Not easy to go AWOL from a set-up like that.'

For a man on the verge of solving a double crime, Burdock felt unreasonably morose. He might not believe in hunches but he still didn't enjoy having them proved wrong. 'Only he did go AWOL, Crewe,' he said tetchily. 'He was found wandering about the campus with straws in his hair. Come on, let's get going.'

'Shouldn't we take Cherry along, sir? If they're as strict as you say, the women-folk might not be easy about talking to strange men.'

'All right, all right. Anything you like, Crewe. Just get a bloody move on.'

CHAPTER TWENTY-FOUR

The following morning, Burdock strode out of the interview room with a face like thunder.

'Get that lot transcribed, would you, Hale. Fast.'

The young constable looked up excitedly. 'Is it true that you've nailed the bleeder, then, sir?'

'Just get on with it, Hale.'

Rattled by the unaccustomed shortness of the inspector's tone, Hale reached for the headphones without further questions. After a minute, though, he stopped typing and scratched his head in bewilderment. He let the recording run on a little further, then turned it off. 'Oh my Gawd, sir,' he said despondently. 'Does it go on like this?'

Burdock surveyed him with grim satisfaction. 'I take it you never went to Sunday school, Hale?'

'Sir?'

'Forget it. Just do the best you can and send Sergeant Crewe up with the transcript when you've finished.'

Crewe brought a message as well as the transcript. 'Jungle drums must be at work already, sir. The Super wants to see you. Congratulations all round, do you reckon?'

Chief Superintendent Fowler was a Londoner and a newcomer to the district. Ten years younger than Burdock and thrustingly ambitious, he had a quick mind and a quicker temper. Burdock's plodding, provincial thoroughness filled him with barely concealed impatience, only exacerbated by the wooden manner which masked Burdock's opinion that the new Super was a jumped-up Johnny with no respect for local knowledge and local ways. Already chafing at the adverse publicity over the delay in solving the baby Gilbert kidnapping, Fowler now wanted decisive action and the media approbation that goes with it.

'All right, Burdock,' he said crisply and without geniality. 'I gather we've cracked the campus murder case. Do I take it that Potter also killed the missing child?'

'It's all circumstantial so far, sir. He has an alibi of sorts for the kidnapping, though not one that would stand up in court.'

Fowler sighed with the testiness of a competent officer held up by a bumbling subordinate. 'Very well, Burdock. Just run me through the details, would you.'

'The accused comes from Bracewell, little village a few miles from Market Monkton. It's a rum place, schizophrenic really. There are Volvo estates parked outside half the houses and the Brethren living in the rest, families with eight or ten kids crammed into a four-roomed cottage. Apparently they came over from Holland in the eighteenth century and they've been living in exactly the same way ever since, with only three or four surnames between them and a dodgy set of genes to match.'

Fowler sighed again. 'Very picturesque, Burdock. Now get to the point, could you.'

'It does have a bearing, sir,' said Burdock with obstinate mildness. 'Anyway, on the Saturday Ben Gilbert disappeared, Potter was supposed to be sitting with his elderly mother to give his sister an afternoon off. She's eighty-six and bed-ridden. Bright as a button, though I think she was rather confused about what we were doing there. She's never had any dealings with the outside world, you see. Anything outside Bracewell might as well be Sodom and Gomorrah. She swore blind that her Enoch had been there all afternoon.'

He could see Fowler twitching with annoyance and ploughed on doggedly. 'It was Sergeant Blossom who discovered the catch. She stayed chatting for an extra few minutes to calm the old girl down and found that she has a memory span of about a quarter of an hour. She would have told us the Angel Gabriel had been there if we'd asked her in the right tone of voice.'

'How long was the sister gone?'

'Long enough for Potter to have got the bus to Oxbourne and back. He'd have been conspicuous, though, with that beard, even if he'd managed a change of clothes. With any luck someone may remember him. We could do with a witness.'

To Superintendent Fowler, luck had nothing to do with policing. 'We could do with a body, Burdock. Which, given the size of the corpse, means either digging up the entire county or cross-questioning Potter until he breaks. What did he say when you interviewed him?'

Burdock pushed a sheaf of paper across the desk. 'He said this, sir.'

Fowler leafed through the pages with growing distaste. 'Tchah, the man's a maniac. Either that or he's hoping to be found unfit to plead. Well, that won't wash here. I want him hammered until he confesses.'

'I thought I might ask Dr Byrd from the university to take a look at his statement, sir. I think there might be more to it than meets the eye.'

'We don't need any smart-arsed psychologists to do our job for us, Burdock.'

'She's in the English department, sir,' said Burdock, dead-pan and meek.

Fowler looked as if he could hardly believe his ears. 'I know there are some coppers who go in for consulting psychics, Burdock. Do I take it you are proposing to call in a literary critic? Good God, man, how do you think that's going to look in the *Daily Mail*?'

'They have these new techniques nowadays, sir. Kind of decoding. Very ingenious. It was Dr Byrd who identified Potter for us, just by reading some anonymous letters he sent to Dr Blair-Guthrie. Fact, I thought I might ask her to take another squint at those as well, now we know a bit more of the background.'

Fowler's attention had already been deflected onto a new target. 'And while we're on the subject, Burdock, do we have any hard evidence that Potter killed Dr Blair-Guthrie, or are you going to tell me that's all circumstantial too?'

'He certainly had a motive for both crimes and he seems to have had the opportunity. We know he left Bracewell without warning sometime on the Tuesday after the kidnapping. He's a joiner by trade and he occasionally does a bit of making and mending for the Volvo set. Seems he'd been paid for a job the day before and instead of putting the money in the communal kitty he just walked off with it. The elders are more shocked by that than by anything else he may have done since. In fact they excommunicated him for it, cast him out in his own absence, so to speak. Otherwise I don't think they'd have co-operated with us at all. They have a long tradition of civil disobedience, apparently. Don't hold with earthly authority in any shape or form. It got them into a lot of trouble during the war. There's an old trout in the village post office who told us all kinds of tales. No one to talk to usually, you see. The Brethren are too holy and the other lot are too snooty, so we got about fifty years of gossip in one batch.

'Anyway, nothing is known of Potter's movements after leaving Bracewell, but Dr Blair-Guthrie was killed a week last Thursday, and Potter turned up on the university campus the following Tuesday in a derelict state, prophesying the destruction of the wicked and mentioning the victim by name. As I see it, there are three real possibilities. If he's completely insane, like as not he's a red herring. If he's only mad part of the time then he's probably our killer. If he's sane then he's either a bloody good liar or we've got the wrong man. If you ask me—'

Fortunately perhaps, Fowler cut him short before he could express an opinion. 'He's clearly a violent and twisted individual, Burdock. You've only got to look at this perverted stuff he comes out with. What about this bit here. "He that goes down to the grave shall come up no more. He consumeth like a rotten thing. If the scourge slay suddenly he will laugh at the trial of the innocent". You don't need to be a literary critic to make sense of that. It's as plain as the nose on your face. He murdered the Gilbert baby and buried him and left him to rot and now he's gloating over the possibility that someone else will go down for it. It's enough in itself to convince a jury. I want to see a bit of action here. I want to be able to reassure the public that the police are on top of this case.'

'Sir.'

'So go and get on with it, Burdock. Fast.'

Burdock went straight downstairs and found Hale. 'Could you tell Crewe I'll be up at the university campus for a bit. Oh and Hale, good work on that statement. It can't have been easy to make sense of all that.'

Hale looked gratified. 'It's a corker, isn't it. I've never heard anything like it. Makes you wonder where he learnt to swear like that, living with a load of holy rollers all his life.'

Burdock arrived on campus still smarting from his encounter with Chief Superintendent Fowler, only to discover that Dr Byrd was in the middle of teaching. The English department administrator, a professional-looking woman with a long-suffering expression, pointed him in the direction of the lecture theatre and advised him to lurk purposefully outside it until his quarry emerged.

'They can be very elusive,' she confided gloomily. 'Even in term time.'

A notice on the door indicated that Dr Byrd was talking about 'Richardson's Clarissa: The Documents in the Case'. Burdock was unacquainted with either Richardson or his

Clarissa but the reference to documents reminded him of his own defiant claims about Dr Byrd's expertise. This seemed a good opportunity to test it out. He slipped through the double doors, which creaked audibly shut behind him, and found himself in a large room packed with long-haired young women all bearing an uncanny resemblance to one another. Dr Byrd was standing on the podium behind a small reading-desk, looking sombre and in control. Burdock was struck yet again by her lack of any trace of feminine softness. No doubt some men would find it rather intriguing. She had exchanged her usual jeans and shirt for an austere ensemble of black trousers and black high-necked sweater, whether in mourning for the dead woman or simply the better to dominate her audience. She was in mid-sentence when Burdock came in. She raised a questioning eyebrow in his direction but her confident delivery barely faltered. Burdock squeezed hastily along a row of industriously scribbling girls and sank into a vacant seat.

So far as he could make out, the lecture seemed to be about a forgery case. The Richardson in question had apparently fabricated an account of a particularly nasty rape, involving the abduction and drugging of the victim, who had subsequently written a series of distraught and crazed letters to her attacker. The thrust of Dr Byrd's argument appeared to concern whether, and if so how, you could tell that these letters had been written by a man. Some of her analysis was couched in language so technical that Burdock was unable to make head or tail of it and some of it was so explicit that it made him shift uneasily in his seat. All around him, the earnest Rapunzels were taking it down, unblushing.

He filed out with the chattering throng and hung around until Dr Byrd emerged carrying a pile of books.

'Hallo, Inspector,' she said sardonically. 'I didn't know you were a student of the eighteenth century.'

'Eighteenth century, eh? That explains why I hadn't heard of the case. But that isn't what I came over to talk about. I wonder if you could cast an eye over something for me. I think it's rather up your street and I should value a second opinion.'

'I'll do my best. Come along to my office.'

'You'll need to know a bit of the background first, though. It's quite a complicated story, I'm afraid.'

'That's fine by me. There's an hour before my next class.'

Dr Byrd listened in silence while Burdock gave her the gist of what he had already told Fowler, and then read through Enoch Potter's statement with her usual speed. When she had finished, she asked curiously, 'What do you want me to tell you?'

'I've already worked out that it comes from the Bible somewhere. I want to know what it means.'

Dr Byrd laughed shortly, sounding more bitter than amused. 'It means, "Oy vey! Oy vey! This I didn't deserve already!" Have you never read the Book of Job?'

'Can't say I have, no. I hope he was a bit more respectable than that other chap you told me about.'

'Oh, you would approve of Job, Inspector. He was so respectable that God decided to subject him to a quality control experiment. So he lost all his property and his children and his health and ended up sitting in an ash heap scratching his boils and arguing with God. Your Enoch Potter obviously knows the whole thing off by heart.'

'Funny idea of God they must have had in those days. So is Potter just bellyaching, would you say, or is he trying to tell us something?'

Dr Byrd looked at him oddly. 'He's trying to tell you that he's innocent, Inspector.'

Burdock felt a surprising sense of relief at having his secret hunch backed up by an independent witness. To hide it he said gruffly, 'Pity he refuses to say so in plain English, then. Do you reckon he's off his head?'

'Oh, I shouldn't think so. People who live with books do tend to think in quotations. And you've got to remember that for someone like Potter the Bible is far more real than his own experience, or rather, it's his only way of explaining his experience to himself. Judging by what you've just told me, that's what he was doing in those anonymous letters as well.'

'How do you mean?'

'I'm afraid we're back with Abraham again. God tested Abraham by telling him to sacrifice his son Isaac, then let him off at the last minute. If you think about it, it's really much the same as the story of Ishmael. You said Enoch Potter changed his son's name from Isaac to Ishmael when he threw his wife out. Superficially, of course, he was saying that the child was an outcast, no longer his, but deeper down, whether he was wholly aware of it or not, he was affirming his own paternity and saying that he wanted the boy to survive, as Hagar's child survived in the wilderness. I should imagine that that's what the letters are really about, Potter's feelings of guilt and remorse and confusion about his own motives. I don't suppose they were really meant to be anonymous, you know. They were letters to his wife. Elspeth would have guessed who they were from and passed them on.'

Burdock felt impressed and discouraged in more or less equal measure. 'If you're right about Potter's statement and we find that he's telling the truth, then we're back where we started. I don't like to think what the Super's going to say.'

'I don't like to think what the parents are going to say. Half the students were only allowed to come back this term because their middle-class mummies and daddies hoped you had the

209

murderer safely behind bars.' She ran her fingers through her inch-long hair, ruffling it up on end. 'Oh shit, how I hate all this! You don't know what it's like on campus now. Fear and suspicion and bloody paranoia and everyone walking on tiptoe in case they step on a landmine. My own colleagues are the worst of the lot, so constipated and English you wouldn't believe. The study of literature is supposed to help you cope with this sort of thing, but it doesn't. You start out longing for vengeance and you end up just wishing you could forget the whole bloody business.'

Burdock made his way glumly back to the station, where Crewe met him, looking maddeningly cheerful.

'We've just had a call from Torquil Guthrie's secretary. He's on his way to Oxbourne now. Oh, and a Professor Morris Kyle phoned from Oxford. He seems to think young Ollie Cresswell has been trying to get in touch with him.'

CHAPTER TWENTY-FIVE

As soon as Torquil Guthrie walked into his office, Burdock realised that he had seen his face before, on the television screen and, more recently, laid out on a mortuary slab. He had his aunt's jutting nose and steely eyes, though his hair was barely streaked with grey and its fierce frizz had been tamed by an expensive barber. His voice was distinctive too. Like his classily well-worn tweed suit, it suggested that he still retained something of the unconscious assumption of privilege which had characterised his family background. Dr Byrd had described Guthrie as a political maverick. Burdock reckoned that he could probably afford to be. However many risks he took, he would never quite manage to step outside the establishment. It was in the tones of a commanding officer rather than a member of the public that he asked Burdock to acquaint him with the details of his aunt's death.

Burdock cleared his throat. 'We have established that Dr Blair-Guthrie arrived back in Oxbourne on Thursday evening of the week before last, when we believe she must have disturbed an intruder in her campus flat. Her body was found lying on the study floor on the Saturday morning by a small boy who had access to the premises in order to feed Dr Blair-Guthrie's cat. The animal had been accidentally killed some days earlier and he wished to remove its food dishes before your aunt returned home.'

'I take it that this small boy was Oliver Cresswell?'

'May I ask how you knew that, sir?'

'My aunt recently rewrote her will and named me as one of the trustees. Oliver Cresswell is the main beneficiary.'

'Yes, I see,' said Burdock, somewhat perplexed. 'Well, as I said, the deceased was discovered in her study, which had been extensively searched. Her neck was broken but she had not been otherwise interfered with. She was still wearing her outdoor clothes, so it's likely that she died soon after arriving at the flat. Hypostasis indicates that the body had not been moved at a later time.'

'According to the papers, you've already caught the bastard who did it. Is that so?'

Burdock felt rather nettled by the sceptical tone of the question, the more so because he was uneasily aware that scepticism might well be in order. He said stiffly, 'We are holding a man in connection with Dr Blair-Guthrie's death, but we are still following up a number of other leads and the investigation is very far from over. Initially we thought that

212

your aunt might have stumbled on a paedophile ring. However, the evidence we were looking for has failed to materialise and our main suspect has since been eliminated.'

Burdock smiled grimly to himself. McBride had been picked up in the north of Scotland the previous day with a vanload of stolen whisky. According to the force in Inverness, he had complained bitterly about police harassment and victimisation when questioned about events in Oxbourne. He had an alibi, though. He had spent the past two months assiduously softening up the stupid floozy who did the accounts at the distillery and on the evening of the murder he had been sitting harmlessly in McDonald's with the wretched woman and her small daughter. Burdock's smile faded at the thought of the child, now in the care of social services.

Torquil Guthrie suddenly stabbed a finger at something behind Burdock's head. 'And would that be one of the leads you're following up?'

Burdock twisted round to see what he was pointing at. It was Oliver Cresswell's drawing of Black Hair and Moustache with their get-away car. He smiled again, indulgently this time.

'Oh, that's just young Oliver Cresswell. He's somehow got it into his head that Dr Blair-Guthrie's cat was kidnapped by a couple of villains in a blue BMW.'

Despite the inspector's dismissive tone, Guthrie seemed oddly disposed to pursue the matter.

'My aunt's cat, you say?'

'So the lad would have us believe.'

'And you don't?'

The question was unexpectedly sharp and it put Burdock on the defensive. 'I know he's supposed to be a bit of a young Einstein, sir, but kids are kids. You can't always believe every word they say.'

'This time I think you should, Inspector. Tell me, where and when did this alleged catnapping take place?'

'The animal turned up in a wood some miles from Oxbourne shortly after the Gilbert baby disappeared. As a matter of fact, it turned up in the Gilbert baby's pram. Shocking waste of police time that cat has caused us, not to mention the headlines. Turned out in the end it was a couple of ten-year-old girls who put it there, which just proves my point really. Kids may be very bright in all sorts of ways, but at that age they just don't understand the nature of evidence.'

Guthrie sighed with testy patience. 'Yes, yes, Inspector, but where did the actual catnapping take place.'

'The alleged catnapping, sir,' said Burdock stolidly. 'Hypothetically speaking, from Dr Blair-Guthrie's flat.'

'In other words, the Cresswell boy claims to have seen the men and the car in that drawing in the vicinity of my aunt's flat during the time she was in San Lorenzo.'

'I suppose you could put it like that, sir, yes.'

'It matters, Inspector. After her return from South America, my aunt had the distinct impression that she was under surveillance. It would never normally have occurred to me to worry about Aunt Eppie. She was a tough old girl who had survived in some pretty hair-raising places. But this time I was concerned enough about her safety to suggest she should write down the details for me, which she did. It now appears that the same men driving the same vehicle were reconnoitring her flat during her absence. The last time I saw my aunt I was just about to take off for Ankara, but I was intending to ask a few discreet questions when I got back to London. It's only fair to warn you that, as soon as my aunt's will is published, I shall be asking those questions in the House.'

Oliver Cresswell seemed more insulted than pleased to find himself being interviewed at last about the men in the blue BMW. He fixed Burdock with an eye as chilly and accusing as Chief Superintendent Fowler's.

'I kept telling people about it and telling people about it and nobody cared a bit. If someone had listened to me in the first place, perhaps it would all have been different. Perhaps Elspeth wouldn't be dead.' His small face pinched itself smaller with the proud determination not to show emotion.

Burdock could tell that any attempt at comfort or denial would be met with furious rejection. He said with awkward heartiness, 'Well, I'm listening to you now, lad, so fire ahead.'

Despite his grief and indignation, Oliver couldn't resist a chance to display his own cleverness. He said slowly, 'I've thought about it a lot since it happened, why they should have wanted to kill Alka-Seltzer like that. I mean, he was fierce but he wasn't a guard dog or anything. He couldn't really have hurt them. Anyway, I think I've worked it out now. Alkie used to sleep on top of the tallboy in Elspeth's study. It reaches nearly to the ceiling, so the burglars – well, actually I suppose they were more like spies, really – wouldn't have known he was there until I came along the corridor and called to him. He always used to jump down and yowl when I did that. I think they must have grabbed him and killed him right away before he could make a noise. They knew how. They did it to Elspeth. Then they must have got out of the window as fast as they could. I saw them just for a second as they were driving away. They took Alka-Seltzer with them because of not leaving evidence behind, but his cushion was knocked on the floor and they forgot about that. It was still warm when I picked it up. They must have thrown his body into Hangman's Wood on their way back to London.'

Burdock was impressed in spite of himself. 'You've got the makings of a real detective, lad, you know that?'

Oliver merely looked his disdain, a look that said louder than any words that he could be a better detective than Burdock any day of the week if he didn't have far more important things to do. Burdock cleared his throat and returned to the matter in hand.

'Those men you saw, now. Do you think you would be able to recognise them if you saw them again?'

Oliver shook his head reluctantly. 'I only got a glimpse of them. One was sort of bald with a moustache and the other one had black hair. That's all I can remember, really.'

'But you're sure you've got the registration number right?'

Oliver looked scornful. 'Of course I am. I always get numbers right.'

'I daresay you do, lad. I daresay you do.' Burdock paused for a moment, then shot out his next question. 'What makes you say they were spies?'

It became apparent that Oliver was thinking fast. 'Well, I suppose because they were proper professionals but they didn't steal anything. It was Elspeth's papers they were after.'

'You said they dumped the cat in Hangman's Wood on their way back to London.'

'So?' The cold eyes in the small, arrogant face were wary now, suspicious.

'How do you know that was where they were going?'

Cornered, Oliver took refuge in one of the traditional defence mechanisms of childhood. He muttered sullenly, 'I just think they were, that's all.'

Stalemate, thought Burdock. But Sergeant Blossom was right; young Oliver was hiding something. Perhaps that Oxford don would have more success than the child psychologist in getting it out of him.

Carefully casual, Burdock said, 'Well, thanks a lot, Oliver, you've been a great help. Oh and before I forget, there's just one other thing. We've had a Professor Morris Kyle on the blower. Name mean anything to you? Apparently he'll be passing through Oxbourne this afternoon and he thought you might like to have a chat.'

CHAPTER TWENTY-SIX

It was only after Professor Kyle's intervention in the case that Oliver finally related what had happened when he discovered Elspeth's body, and even then he didn't tell it all. Some of it involved feelings he didn't want to talk about and some of it was private for quite a different reason.

'Elspeth told me always to remember that the things of the tribe are secret. She said that's what Kainu boys are taught and I had to learn it as well, cross my heart and hope to die. It's called a tabco, something that you mustn't ever break. She said there was stuff she never put in her book because it was secret to the tribe.'

'About her own initiation, you mean? Yes, I believe that that is so. Not all anthropologists are so scrupulous; indeed I am not wholly certain that, given such an opportunity, I should be so myself. But you can tell me the general outline, I take it? I had to promise the police that I would urge you to help them to the best of your ability. As I am sure you are already aware, it is highly probable that her recent transactions with regard to the Kainu people have a bearing on Dr Blair-Guthrie's death.'

As he gave Professor Kyle his carefully edited account, Oliver found himself remembering with painful vividness the moments following his finding of the body. Automatically, as he had done the last time he had been in that room, he had walked to the window and looked out, half expecting to see the blue BMW speeding away. There was nothing there. He had shut his eyes and leaned his forehead against the cold glass of the windowpane. He had felt unnaturally calm, but it was as if everything had gone into slow motion including his brain. Think, he told himself urgently. You've got to think. You're a man now, a man of the tribe. You have to decide what to do.

And then he remembered; the ritual was not yet complete. The rest of the ceremony had been performed with another boy as proxy, but the invocation to the great lizard spirit had to come from his own mouth. It was for this that he had practised so hard, playing and replaying the recording that Elspeth had given him until the mysterious words were burned into his memory, reciting his own part of the dialogue until he could reproduce every syllable, every inflection. He would not be a man of the tribe until he had spoken those words and Elspeth had put the manhood beads around his neck. And now Elspeth was dead and all that effort had been in vain. He knew that this mattered terribly; more than anything had ever mattered. More than his own disappointment and loss. More even than Elspeth's death. Elspeth had entrusted the safety of the tribe to him and he had failed. There was nothing he could do.

He walked back across the room and looked down at the dead woman. Though she lay in an ungainly heap, her face was stern, almost accusing. She had not been surprised or frightened when she died. Her eyes stared up at him, glassy and unseeing. You were supposed to close the eyelids, he remembered. People even used to put coins on them to weigh them down. Or perhaps it was to pay for the dead person's passage into the spirit world. Was that where Elspeth was now, in the spirit world among the ancestors? But she hadn't just died, somebody had killed her. You weren't supposed to touch anything at the scene of the crime before the police arrived.

Oliver turned uncertainly towards the desk, where an old landline telephone stood. He picked up the receiver, then put it down again. If he called the police, they would just send him straight home like a little kid. And then they would zip Elspeth up inside a big black bag, like the ones you sometimes saw on the television news, and take her away, and it would all be over. And it couldn't be. It simply couldn't. His face began to screw itself up with the onset of tears. Like a little kid, when what he needed was to be a man. Desperately he said out loud, 'Help me! Please, please, somebody help me!'

Even as he spoke, he remembered that, when Elspeth had first begun to prepare him for his initiation into the tribe, she had told him, 'If anything happens, I mean, if for some reason you should find yourself in need of help or advice, you should get in touch with my nephew Torquil or with Morris Kyle at Oxford.'

As he had told Morgan, Oliver didn't need to memorise numbers. The phone numbers Elspeth had given him were written in his head. He chewed at his knuckles while he considered his options. There was little point in phoning Torquil Guthrie. Even if he managed to get through to him, and Oliver could see that a small boy phoning the House of Commons might find it hard to have his call taken seriously, there was no way that a Liberal Democrat MP could help in this particular emergency. But Professor Kyle was an anthropologist. He might know what Oliver should do.

The phone rang only three times, then he heard a courteous and scholarly voice saying, 'Professor Kyle is unable to answer your call at present as he will be in Papua New Guinea until the start of term. Please leave a message after the tone.'

Oliver said passionately, 'Oh bloody, *bloody* hell!' and banged the receiver down. He started to walk back towards Elspeth's body, picking his way through the mounds of clothing and papers on the floor. 'You're an ancestor spirit now,' he thought. 'You have to help me. There isn't anyone else.'

Something brightly coloured was lying half-hidden beside the open suitcase. Oliver stooped and picked it up. A bunch of gaudy parrot feathers fastened to a half-moon of shell decorated with bone pendants and jaguar claws hung from a string of black and scarlet nau seeds. He was holding the manhood beads, which the shaman had filled with power in a secret place in the forest and Elspeth had gone to South America to bring back for him. Oliver turned them over in his hands. He knew now what he was going to do. 'This isn't a game,' Elspeth had told him. He would have to make it as real as he could. There was a felt-tip pen clipped into his blazer pocket and he would need a mirror as well. There was one in the bathroom. He laid the beads down beside Elspeth's body and went to prepare himself for the ceremony.

The boy who came back into the room was naked and walked very proud and tall as befits a son of the tribe on the day of his initiation. His cheekbones were painted with the swirling lines of tattooing which distinguish the men of the lizard clan and he carried a Kainu spear which usually hung above the hall table. He crouched beside Elspeth and without hesitation took her right hand and held it against his forehead. A distant part of his mind registered that it was chilly but not stiff. Rigor mortis, that was how the police worked out the time of death. He pushed the thought away before it disturbed his concentration. He had played Elspeth's recording so often that it was easy to make her voice speak inside his head, repeating the opening words of the ritual. The difficult part was switching off the voice as he straightened up to make the responses, but somehow he managed it. When the moment came, he folded Elspeth's cold fingers round the necklace and held them there as he pulled it over his head. He stood up and raised his spear and his voice rose triumphantly in the final invocation, as high and pure as an English choirboy chanting the psalms. The ceremony was over; he was a man.

Soberly he went to wash his face and put on his clothes. He had done the best he could. He would have to wait until Professor Kyle came back from New Guinea to find out whether it really counted but at least he had tried. And now there was only one thing left to be done. Oliver found himself suddenly reluctant to do it. You dialled 999 and asked for the police and as like as not they didn't believe you, and anyhow you didn't know how to tell them that Elspeth had been murdered without starting to cry like a little kid. So in the end it had seemed easier to phone Morgan instead.

He had had time before she arrived to hang the spear back on the wall and bury the precious beads deep in his blazer pocket. He hadn't wanted any awkward evidence of what he had been doing.

'Only I forgot about the photograph, and they sort of got the wrong idea.'

'So I gather. Understandable, given the circumstances. Though the good Inspector is plainly a student of life, his knowledge of ritual practices could hardly be expected to extend that far.'

'It's my mother who really got worked up about it.'

'You would be well advised to clear up the misunderstanding before she learns the terms of Dr Blair-Guthrie's will.'

'Do you think that still counts? I mean, perhaps I did it all wrong. I was only guessing.'

'Oh yes, I should imagine that it does. I'm no expert on the Kainu, as you know. My field is kinship systems in Papua New Guinea. However, I have been reading up the literature since Dr Blair-Guthrie first consulted me and, as I recall, there is a legend about the trickster Karu-roa who speaks to his son from beyond the grave.'

'And tells him how to use the green lizard skin to cheat his enemy. Elspeth told me that story.'

'You said that when you performed the ceremony you made Dr Blair-Guthrie speak inside your head. Would you say that you actually heard her?'

'I made the sound of her voice. It was like playing the recording. Anyway, perhaps she heard me in the spirit world. I mean, she gave me the beads.'

'She was an atheist, of course. A most pragmatic and rational person.'

'That doesn't mean that I have to be.'

'No, indeed. In any case, I do not think you need worry. The San Lorenzan authorities will not care about the validity of the ceremony. Legally speaking, it is enough that you are Dr Blair-Guthrie's heir. And I think you will find that the precedent of Karu-roa's son will enable the chief and the shaman to accept your initiation. After all, it is wholly in their own interests to do so.'

'You mean, Karu-roa's son was allowed to cheat and so will they?'

'They will not put it to themselves in those terms, of course. They will simply draw on elements in their belief system which will enable them to accept you as a member of the tribe. Well, that clears everything up, I think. There's just one other small point. The police mentioned something about a painting of a cat. They said you put it next to the body.'

Oliver's faced closed up defensively and he said nothing. The professor looked at him with the detached curiosity he normally brought to fieldwork interviews in New Guinea.

'Did it perhaps have some ritual significance? I'm not very well informed about Kainu funerary customs.'

Oliver flushed. For a moment he looked both haughty and furious. Then, in as offhand a voice as he could manage, he said, 'Just, I thought he would be ... well, company.'

CHAPTER TWENTY-SEVEN

Inspector Burdock had not reached his present rank without learning to put up with disappointment. Indeed, he was in the habit of pointing out, in an avuncular way, to over-ambitious junior officers that you only had to look at the clear-up rates to realise that real life detective work is eighty-five per cent frustration and if you want to change the odds, go and audition for *Midsomer Murders*. So it was not so much the frustration of his own efforts to track down the occupants of the blue BMW that stung, it was the form in which that frustration came. During the years they had worked together, Sergeant Crewe had on occasion seen the inspector bad-tempered or out of sorts. He had never before seen him in the cold black rage in which he returned from Chief Superintendent Fowler's office.

After eyeing him with wary sympathy for a few moments, Crewe asked tentatively, 'What was the Super on about this time, sir? Trouble, was it?'

He was rewarded by an audible snarl from Burdock. 'Only a potential bloody miscarriage of justice, Crewe. That's what the Super was bleeding well on about.'

'Sir?'

Burdock snapped into chilly formality. 'Potter is being charged with Dr Blair-Guthrie's murder. He'll appear in court on Monday morning. Oh, and he's to be remanded into police custody so we can hammer him some more about the kidnapping. Fowler's busy briefing the press.'

'But I thought...'

'Well, stop bloody thinking. We're not being asked to think.'

'I mean... what about that car we were tracing?'

'That, Crewe, was simply a figment of Dr Blair-Guthrie's over-heated imagination.'

'It can't have been, surely. The kid saw it too.'

'Then she must have put the idea into his impressionable little head, mustn't she, Crewe? And what's more, while she was concocting this paranoid fantasy, the vehicle registration number she happened to pick on just happened to be an ever so sensitive one. We've been warned off. At the very highest level.'

'But... I mean, why on earth...?'

Burdock smiled grimly. 'Just because she was paranoid, Crewe, doesn't mean she wasn't under surveillance.'

'But she was just a harmless little old lady, wasn't she?'

'Apparently not. But we can forget about all that because

we've already got the poor mad bastard who did it. So all we have to do now is bully and badger him until he breaks down and confesses and that will be everything nicely sewn up.'

Crewe found himself unable to meet Burdock's eye. He glanced away, embarrassed by a shared sense of guilt by association. Staring unhappily at the floor, he ventured quietly, 'Stitched up, do you mean, sir?'

'That's about the size of it, Crewe, yes.'

'What are you going to do about it?'

Burdock shrugged. 'Far as I can see, there's bugger all I *can* do. I can't blow the whistle on Fowler and he's made it perfectly plain that if I don't at least appear to toe the line he'll take me off the case. I'll have one more go at interviewing Potter and I'll get Dr Greenwood to take another look at him. I'm as certain as I can be that he didn't do it, but if I can't get some sort of sense out of him about his whereabouts at the time of the murder then he's going to go down for it, guilty or not.'

In the bleak pause that followed, Crewe looked around for something comforting to say. 'What about the Ben Gilbert case, sir? *He* can't have been abducted by Special Branch thugs or whoever it was did in the old lady. And Potter had a motive for that too, didn't he? So perhaps he's guilty of something after all.'

Burdock sighed, weary and defeated. 'I don't know, Crewe. I honestly don't know.'

Dr Henry Greenwood had been a police surgeon for over thirty years. He was a lean, loose-jointed man with the melancholy face of an out-of-work comedian above a flamboyantly drooping bow-tie. He exuded an air of patient and unexpectant calm which made people talk to him. Foul-mouthed drunks bruised and bleeding after pub brawls, youthful joyriders shivering in the aftermath of multiple pile-ups, women who had knifed their abusive husbands or strangled their new-born babies, all found themselves confiding in Dr Greenwood. He paid the same mild attention to all their stories, however banal, incoherent, obscene or horrifying the words in which they were conveyed, and for some of the tellers it was the first time that they had perceived their lives as more than random chaos without meaning or shape.

From Enoch Potter he elicited nothing, not a word or a reaction, nor even a moment of eye contact. It was not a question of obstinacy or refusal. The man seemed to be marooned in some lost place beyond the possibility of speech or human fellowship. Enoch had not spoken at all since the dramatic outburst that Burdock had shown to Dr Byrd, and the successive magistrate's warrants which had prolonged his time in police custody had led to nothing more in the way of evidence than repeated recordings of Burdock's frustrated questions punctuated by long stretches of silence. Burdock's latest attempt was no more successful and he was constrained by the knowledge that Fowler was expecting him to incriminate Potter, not to plug away at trying to gain his co-operation. His conversation with Dr Greenwood was none too encouraging either.

'Is he off his head, do you reckon, or is he just holding out on us? His lot don't have any truck with the law, or with doctors either come to that.'

Dr Greenwood shook his head. 'I don't think he's mentally ill, or not in the sense you mean, anyway. I suppose you could describe him as suffering from terminal bereavement.'

Burdock was puzzled, as much by the tone as the words. 'Terminal? Like dying of a broken heart, you mean? Bit fanciful that, isn't it?'

'No, not really. People who find themselves in police custody usually have something to lose; their liberty, their reputation, their livelihood, perhaps even their closest relationships. But they still have the fragments of their community and their world, the things that make us human. Potter has lost everything.'

Burdock remembered Dr Byrd's scripture lesson. 'Like Job, you mean?'

'Far worse. Job had a wife to nag him and friends to argue with and a sense of his own innocence to sustain him.'

'So you do think Potter is guilty, then?' Despite himself, Burdock couldn't keep a tinge of hope out of his voice. Perhaps this bloody awful mess was going to tidy itself up after all.

Dr Greenwood smiled mournfully. 'In the middle ages they would have described his condition as tristitia. The sin of despair. Nowadays I suppose you would call it severe reactive depression. You used to see the same thing in children's wards in the old days when the parents were forbidden to visit. The child would feel it must be impossibly wicked to deserve such desertion. The symptoms could be almost like autism.'

The flicker of hope died out. Burdock found himself back on the hook and the feeling of let-down exasperated him. 'It's homicide I'm concerned with here,' he said sharply, 'not the state of his wretched soul. Is Potter guilty of killing an old woman and a baby or isn't he? That's all I want to know.'

Dr Greenwood sighed. 'As to that, I can't tell you, but I suspect it's hardly going to matter. If the case goes to trial, he'll be found unfit to plead. Barring a miracle, he's going to be spending the rest of his life in a secure mental hospital.'

Fowler's press conference achieved its intended effect. On Monday morning, reporters and photographers were massed outside the magistrates court, the unusual gathering of telephoto lenses alerting a growing crowd of local people to what was about to take place. By the time the police van arrived, the crowd had become a mob. Burdock had failed to anticipate trouble on anything approaching this scale. Nothing like it had ever happened in Oxbourne before. For a few minutes, while he phoned for reinforcements, the crowd surrounded the van, their voices rising in a baying chant as they hammered on the bodywork, rocking the vehicle with the savagery of their onslaught. Meanwhile the satisfied press was busily recording the blood-lust they had helped to provoke.

Finally, with the crowd held back by a police cordon, Potter was bundled out of the van swathed in a blanket. What happened next was probably Burdock's fault. It had not occurred to him that this sequence of events might be misunderstood by a prisoner who had never watched the television news. Stifled and panic-stricken, Potter struggled wildly and managed to break free for an instant from the concealing cloth. A dozen cameras clicked, eleven of them just too late, as the chanting filled the air again, mindless and terrifying and reduced now to a single reiterated word, which next morning would become the stuff of national headlines.

Sister Maxwell was one of the few people in the country not to have seen them. She usually skimmed through the *Telegraph* over breakfast in her staff flat, but the previous evening the night sister had suddenly gone down with appendicitis and Sister Maxwell had had to work a double shift. She should by rights have been off duty and asleep by now, but she was still bustling about the ward because she was worried about Mr Gilbert. He had been looking increasingly haggard since little Ben's disappearance, but this morning his yellowish skin was drawn tightly over the angles of his skull and he was shivering as if he had malaria. Sister Maxwell was not normally given to flights of fancy, but when she took him in his morning coffee he had looked to her like a soul in hell. More to the point, he had looked like a man who was in no state to spend the afternoon in theatre. Sister Maxwell had felt so concerned that she had lingered, bracing herself to say something to him when she went back to collect the empty cup.

James Gilbert, meanwhile, was sitting at his desk with a newspaper he would never normally have bought spread out in front of him. Earlier that morning, he had watched with barely controlled impatience as Libby pored desperately over a pile of what the literate middle classes mean by the morning paper. It filled him with anger and with something that was almost contempt to see her searching the restrained accounts of yesterday's court appearance for some clue which would explain why their son had died. For himself, he had known without needing to look that all she would find was a banal recital of already-known facts. Enoch Potter, aged fifty-three, had been charged in Oxbourne magistrates court with the murder of Dr Elspeth Blair-Guthrie and remanded into police custody for further questioning about the disappearance and presumed unlawful killing of Benjamin Gilbert, aged four months. Reporting restrictions had not been lifted. It was barely even a story, devoid as it was of detail and human interest, though the picture editors had been able to pep it up a bit with photographs of the crowd outside the courthouse. He and Libby had seen that crowd already on last night's television news and heard the rasping, concerted yell of 'Monster! Monster! Monster!'

That word screamed up at him now from the tabloid page in front of him, above the image of a crazed, contorted face, the eyes fixed and staring in what could have been either frenzy or terror. James Gilbert had bought the paper on his way to the hospital, choosing a newsagent where no one would recognise him – a furtive act like the illicit purchase of pornography. The need, the compulsion, to see the face of the man who had stolen Ben and killed him (How? Strangled him? Smothered him? Worse than that?) had felt to him like a source of shame. He had hastily folded the paper so that the face was concealed and hidden it away in his briefcase.

He had been staring at that face for almost half an hour. At first glance it had looked like the embodiment of evil, but the more he gazed at it, the more it had broken down into a dirty mess of newsprint dots, until at last he had looked right through it into a swirling void which showed him that he himself was nothing and would understand nothing for there was nothing left to understand. It was perfectly clear what had happened. Potter had murdered Ben because he himself had operated on Potter's child. Motivation didn't matter. Those were the facts. He might as well have lifted the knife to kill his own son. This faceless face, this mask, was his own.

Nursing is not a profession which encourages any respect for privacy. Sister Maxwell's knock on the door was a relic of hospital feudalism, a formal acknowledgement of his status as a consultant surgeon. It was followed, without pause or invitation, by Sister Maxwell herself. Instinctively, James Gilbert shifted a file, as if at random, to hide at least the lurid one word headline from her view. Sister Maxwell advanced towards the desk, her hand outstretched for the untouched cup and a look of nannyish admonition on her face. She was opening her mouth to tell him that he had let his coffee get cold again when she paused. She moved round to peer over his shoulder at the wild eyes staring out from under the edge of the black plastic folder. James Gilbert felt his guts contract in a spasm of pure rage. But when she spoke, her words were not the ones he was expecting.

'Do you know, I could swear I'd seen that face before somewhere.' She hovered behind him, pondering this minor mystery. 'Oh, of course, I've got it now. That's the man in the black hat. Good heavens, what on earth is he doing in the paper?'

She leaned closer to read the sensation-mongering caption. 'Cult member and accused killer Enoch Potter. Is this the monster who snatched Baby Ben?'

If Inspector Burdock had only known it, that question was about to be answered. Two nervous teenage girls, one clutching a copy of the *Sun*, were boarding the bus to Oxbourne. Apart from their matching navy school blazers they were an ill-assorted pair. The giggly one had gold earrings and flaking nail varnish and a bum-length, bum-tight mini-skirt. Her incipient beauty, already starting to shine through the fog of adolescent discontent, was marred by the ugly metal band which confined her front teeth. The shy one had escaped the orthodontics which had temporarily disfigured most of her classmates, though this fact was not in evidence since her lips were pinched tightly together in an expression of scared determination. She wore a long print dress under her blazer and her braided hair was demurely covered by a black headscarf.

When the bus arrived, the two slid hurriedly into a back seat, anxious not to be noticed and challenged. As they rocked their way through the leafy countryside they conversed intently in low voices.

'Just wait till I tell my mum I spent the morning down the cop-shop. She'll probably think I've been done for under-age drinking.'

'Will they... do you think they'll tell our parents?'

'Doesn't matter if they do, does it? It's not as if we've just bunked off for the hell of it.'

'It's not that. But if I have to appear in court ...'

'If you don't mind me saying so, it's funny your folks are so shy of the cops when they're supposed to be so holy and everything.'

The other girl flushed. 'It's just that we're not meant to judge others. Vengeance is mine, saith the Lord.'

'That's barmy. I mean, I'm sorry, but it is, Kerry. What about your uncle practically divorcing your auntie just 'cos she took her kid to the doctor? Is that judging other people or what?'

Her companion hesitated, then said in a nervous rush, 'All right, perhaps he shouldn't have. Perhaps he should have gone with her. I'm sure Mother thinks so, though she doesn't dare say. At least then there wouldn't have been all this trouble.'

'But religion is barmy anyway when you think. I mean,

they got up to all sorts in the Bible. Adultery, incest, the lot. And think of your name, even. Old Fishface said in RE that it means horn of eye make-up, but I bet your mum would have fifty fits if you borrowed my mascara.'

The other girl ducked her head and said nothing. Her friend looked at her with not unkindly curiosity.

'Do you really believe in all that, Kerry? I mean, really?'

Looking earnestly at her clasped hands, the girl said slowly, 'No, I don't. I don't believe Aunt Naomi should have allowed her son to die the way my little brother did. But I don't believe in the things of this world either. Look at the stuff in that newspaper, even. It's horrible. You can't blame the Brethren for wanting to stay separate from all that. Only you can't stay separate. You just can't. If I don't say anything, it will be all my fault if that baby is never found. And his parents need him back, I know they do.' She hesitated, then added in an unhappy whisper, 'Even if it's only to bury him.'

'Cheer up. You're doing your best. I bet God will understand. Want a ciggie? No, it's OK, I was only joking. Look, I think this is our stop.'

Ten minutes later, Mary Blossom knocked on Burdock's door. She was looking amused about something.

'We've got a Miss Kerenhappuch Cordwainer and friend down in reception, sir. Apparently she wants a word with you about her uncle.'

240

CHAPTER TWENTY-EIGHT

Octavia Castlemain seldom tried to involve her husband Richard in her philanthropic schemes, though all too often he found himself living with the consequences of her compulsive urge to set the world to rights. An experienced passive resister in his absent-minded way, Professor Castlemain barricaded himself into his study behind a mound of books and a more impenetrable barrier of abstruse and abstract scholarship. However, on this occasion there was no escape. The previous day, Dr Greenwood's wife had come into the Oxfam shop, in search, as she said, of a complete set of gent's clothing.

'Henry has brought home one of his lame ducks again. So if you'd like to help me rummage, Octavia, I'll be eternally grateful. I've had to guess the sizes, I'm afraid. He's a terribly prudish little man. He'd probably faint dead away on the carpet if I offered to measure his inside leg.'

Sharp, clever, irreverent and out-spoken, Miriam Greenwood was well aware that she figured in Octavia's life both as crony and as rival. They had plotted and sparred together on half a dozen committees. As they sorted through the racks of second-hand shirts and jackets, she teased Octavia by holding back the name of her unexpected guest in order to reveal it in a final throw-away line. Octavia retaliated by offering Richard's services.

'It'll be no trouble, dear. He has to go up to town in any case, to examine a thesis or something. He'll just need to set out a little earlier, that's all.'

So in the end it was Richard Castlemain who drove Enoch Potter to London. Disguised in his Oxfam shop garments and with his hair and beard neatly trimmed, Enoch was hardly recognisable as the Old Testament patriarch who had echoed the lamentations of Job. Shorn of his flowing mane and forced to suffer the officious kindness of strangers, he seemed both bewildered and diminished. Richard's genuine lack of any desire to add to that burden of kindness was a greater mercy than he could possibly have known. The two men passed the journey in mutually uncomprehending silence and parted outside the hospital with a brief handshake. Enoch was left standing alone outside the huge building, among the bustle of ambulances and taxis and visitors buying flowers, trying to summon up the courage to go in. All-seeing and impartial as the eye of God, the security cameras looked down on his distress. No one else so much as spared a glance at the nondescript little man hesitating in front of the flower stall. Miriam Greenwood had done her work well.

The security cameras too had done their work. Installed only a few months earlier, following the nation-wide panic aroused by the abduction of an hour-old baby from a London maternity ward, they had enabled Burdock to eliminate Potter from the investigation in a way the Chief Superintendent couldn't possibly argue with. While Elspeth Blair-Guthrie was dying at the hands of an unknown assailant, Enoch Potter, unmistakable in the broad-brimmed black hat which had attracted the attention of Sister Maxwell, had been pacing up and down outside the hospital where his son was lying. It was evident from the camera footage that he had haunted the place for a couple of weeks, never daring to go inside. It must have been a nightmarish experience, Burdock thought. A sojourn in the city of dreadful night, friendless, confused, probably sleeping rough, knowing he could never return to the Brethren, too ashamed of his divided feelings to be prepared to say later where he had spent those missing days. And then the attempt to seek help from Dr Blair-Guthrie, not knowing she was already dead. Followed by arrest and detention and Fowler's readiness to send him down to cover up a politically embarrassing crime. A crime that Burdock now knew he would never be allowed to solve. Still, at least the Superintendent had been cheated of his sacrificial lamb. That was something.

'Escaped out of Fowler's snare, as you might say,' he said with grim satisfaction to Sergeant Crewe, who looked at him rather blankly in reply. Dr Byrd would have got the allusion, thought Burdock wistfully. Pity he couldn't have tried it on her.

'And all through the power of our noble and disinterested press,' said Crewe. 'Makes you sick, doesn't it? I bet the Super thinks you sneaked them that photo opportunity on purpose.'

'So I would have done, if I'd thought of it,' said Burdock stoutly.

'I'm surprised at the niece, though. A mousy little thing like that, looking as if butter wouldn't melt, Cherry said. And all the time she was reading the tabloids on the sly.'

'I don't think she was, you know. It was her chum who worked it all out. The brassy one. Seems she keeps a diary. She's the type.'

Young Kerenhappuch Cordwainer had proved to be an unexpectedly composed and intelligent witness. She had not come forward before because she had been unaware that a baby had been kidnapped, let alone that her uncle might be a suspect. Since his casting out, his name was never mentioned among the Brethren. Like the other kids, she had been at school in Market Monkton when Burdock had questioned the villagers. She remembered the day when Ben was taken because they'd had a session with the careers teacher the previous afternoon.

She was certain about the date because her friend Samantha had annoyed Miss Borthwick by saying she was going to be a model and had written up the subsequent row in her diary. She herself had shyly confessed that she had ambitions to go to college, the first time she had dared to mention this forbidden and dangerous plan.

'Miss Borthwick said I ought to stay on and do my A levels and I should have a talk with my parents, only that's not so easy. I think Mother knows, really, but it'll be hard on her. There's bound to be trouble with the elders, and anyway when young people leave the community they don't generally come back. I wanted to talk to my Gran about it. She's so old and not quite with herself that you can tell her things, you see. Things you couldn't tell anyone else. Only when I went round, my uncle Enoch was there so I just made the tea and read the Bible to Gran for a bit. That piece in the newspaper that Sammy showed me, saying my uncle might have taken away a baby, it gave the day and time when it was stolen. Gran wouldn't remember, but I know my Uncle Enoch couldn't have done it because he was there with us. He couldn't have done it anyway, not a terrible thing like that. I know the Brethren think he's a lost soul, but he's a good man, my uncle. He wouldn't ever do anything to harm anyone. Not if he could help it.'

Standing beside the flower stall, Enoch Potter thought about the woman whose life he had maimed. He had never given her flowers. It was she who had brought them in from the garden in careful posies and arranged them in a blue jug. It was a strange thing to him that flowers could be bought and sold instead of being coaxed from the earth. The rose of Sharon, he thought, the lily of the valley. But these flowers, tightly packed and cellophane wrapped, were part of the vain traffic of Babylon, things that seemed made rather than grown. And then he noticed, among the falsely perfect carnations and the roses whose petals would never unfurl, a single bunch of white narcissi. The delicate flower-heads, half open, already breathed their honeyed scent which spoke to him of new beginnings and all the freshness of spring. Slowly, like someone speaking his first hesitant words in a new language, he felt in his pocket for a handful of coins.

Naomi, sitting by her sleeping child, saw him enter the room, her husband and yet a stranger, gingerly holding the wrapped blooms. He stopped on the far side of the incubator and stood looking down at their son.

After a moment he said, 'Isaac.'

Naomi closed her eyes, unable to look him in the face. She said, 'I lied to you, Enoch. Can you forgive me for that?'

Her humility, the lack of reproaches, amazed him. His head bowed over the gently breathing infant, he recited the bitter lesson that his captivity had taught him.

'The Lord has shown me in these last days that the sin was only mine. I wanted the boy to live but I was not willing to take the burden of it on my conscience. So I cast you out unjustly, and now I am justly cast out.'

Her reply fell softly into the charged space between them. 'The Lord has been very merciful to us, Enoch. He has lifted His hand from our firstborn.'

'Only how shall we live, alone in the wilderness?'

She stretched out her hands to him, suddenly filled with a radiance of certainty which lit up her face. 'We have each other. And the child. We will find out a way.'

CHAPTER TWENTY-NINE

The funeral of the Hon Elspeth Blair-Guthrie, MA Edin, DPhil Oxon, took place, inappropriately enough, beneath the serene fan vaulting of Oxbourne Abbey. This venue had been carefully chosen, not only as one of the few public spaces in Oxbourne large enough to hold the anticipated crowd of mourners but also as the latest battleground in Torquil Guthrie's campaign to publicise what he was now convinced were the real circumstances of his aunt's murder. Elspeth herself had been a staunch atheist ever since her Presbyterian childhood and had she died a natural death her passing would have been marked by a quiet cremation, followed in due course by a series of commemorative lectures on anthropological subjects. However she had, as Morgan kept reminding herself, been a firm believer in the principle that whoever wills the end wills the means. Much as she might have deplored both the fuss and the Anglican setting, she would certainly have approved of her nephew's tactics.

Morgan would, in any case, have gone to Elspeth's funeral dry-eyed and angry. It was because of the television cameras that she dressed for it with such care. In the charade they were about to enact, everything would carry a hidden subtext, even her own performance. Torquil had struck a tacit bargain with the Vicar over the arrangements for the service. Religion would be kept to a decent minimum and political or otherwise contentious topics would be touched on obliquely, if at all. Instead, the colleagues and friends of the dead woman would convey their sense of her work and personality through a programme of short readings. Morgan had not needed to rehearse her chosen poem; she already knew it by heart. Instead she spent an hour assembling her image in front of the bedroom mirror, putting together the different blacks of silk and velvet and leather, clipping on her most dramatic ear-rings, combing back her spiky hair. The effect she finally achieved was at once funereal, aggressive and chic. She came downstairs with a conscious clicking of boot-heels to find Lin, her beauty thinly disguised by the dowdy two-piece she usually wore to private views, waiting patiently in the hall.

By the time they reached the centre of Oxbourne, the congregation was already assembling and it took Morgan ten minutes to find a parking space. The streets around the abbey were crowded with cars and a steady stream of people were making their way towards the great west door. Among the sober throng Morgan noticed Rupert Allison toting the sleeping Joshua and hung back in order to avoid him. Right now she was in no mood for babies. Gradually, however, she became aware that the crowd was full of them. Larger offspring had been left with child-minders or grandparents, but since the kidnapping Oxbourne had become a place where babies, like young chimpanzees, spent their entire waking lives clasped to a parental bosom. Most of her English Department colleagues would be at the funeral and so, Morgan grimly calculated, would Douglas Henderson's Gawain and John Bailey's Emily and Geoff Wood's Fergus. As they turned the corner towards the abbey, she encountered Rosalind Gilbert, looking pale and stressed and wheeling the swathed bundle that was Persephone Jane. She greeted Morgan distractedly, with most of her attention on the television vans which filled the abbey precinct.

'Oh, Morgan, hello. Oh dear, it looks like a film set over there, doesn't it. I suppose I'd better take the pram apart out here. Then I can just slip in quietly.' She unhooked one end of the string of brightly coloured plastic beads which spanned the carrycot frame and folded back the blanket, transfixing Morgan with a sudden disagreeable memory of dead cat. It was almost a relief to see that the occupant of the pram was human and dribbling and dressed in white frills. Rosalind fished her out and for a moment seemed about to thrust her into Morgan's arms, but the look on Morgan's face made her think better of it. Instead she stood uncertainly, clutching the wriggling infant and looking from Morgan to the pram and back again.

Morgan said hastily, 'Let Lin do it. She's the mechanical one.'

Indeed, Lin was already bending over the pram, pensively reattaching the string of beads.

Rosalind said loudly, 'Oh, don't do that, Lin. I have to put her in again, you see. If you could just undo these clips at the sides.'

Morgan knew it was pointless to lose her temper when someone yelled at Lin while not giving her a chance to lip-read. Apart from anything else, Lin was in no need of her protection. She worked off her irritation by signing, 'She wants you to take the bloody thing to bits, lover.'

Rosalind hovered about while she did so, nervous and effusive.

'Oh, that's wonderful. Thank you so much. And the undercarriage sort of folds flat if you lift that bit there, look.'

As Rosalind finally scurried off towards a side door with her infant back in its deconstructed cot, Torquil Guthrie arrived in the precinct, meticulously tailored and barbered and squiring the octogenarian Baroness Buckhaven. Oliver Cresswell, accompanied by his mother, walked on the other side of the wheelchair. The venerable Labour peeress had been a fellow student of Elspeth's at Somerville. More to the point, her craggy face and fighting reputation made the little group a magnet for the cameras. It was plain that Daphne had intended Ollie to look like a child virtuoso. To Morgan, the dark suit and violin case gave him more the air of a diminutive mafia hit-man. His hair had been slicked down with gel and he was wearing a bow-tie. Daphne herself was in exaggerated mourning including a hat with a veil.

The cameras would have homed in on Ollie in any case. He was currently enjoying a wholly new kind of celebrity. When Elspeth had decided to involve him in her plans, it had been clear to her that maximum publicity would be the best safeguard both for him and for the Kainu, so his trip to London for the reading of the will had included several carefully vetted interview sessions, leading to articles in the quality press and even an appearance on *Newsnight*. Daphne's shock at discovering that her son had been secretly initiated into a South American tribe in order to inherit the tribal land had been sensibly assuaged not only by all the media attention but also by the other provisions of Elspeth's will. To ensure that Daphne would not repudiate the legacy on Oliver's behalf, she had also left him part of a rather grand crescent in Georgian Edinburgh, inherited from her mother who, it emerged, had been the only daughter of a beer baron before marrying into the impoverished highland aristocracy.

Oliver on *Newsnight* had been unmistakably Oliver, facing a genial Kirsty Wark with chilly disdain. Invited to describe his initiation, he had flatly declined.

'I don't want to talk about that. It's private.'

'Well then, perhaps you could tell us what it was all in aid of.'

'It was because the gold prospectors were going to steal the bit of forest where the Kainu live and the government was going to let them do it. So Aapuulo – he's the chief – asked Elspeth to buy the land, with all the proper bits of paper, so no one else could take it away. She was part of the tribe anyway because she had helped them once before, so that meant it really still belonged to them, you see. Only she was getting pretty old, and she knew some spies were after her too, so she asked me to be in the tribe as well in case she... Well, in case she wasn't there anymore.'

'Dr Blair-Guthrie told you about the spies?'

'No, of course not. Don't be silly. Grown-ups don't talk to kids about stuff like that.'

'So what put the idea into your head, Oliver?'

'I put two and two together. And they didn't come to five either, if that's what you're going to say. I can add up, you know.'

His interviewer accepted defeat and tried a different tack.

'So what are your duties as guardian of the tribal territory?'

I don't have any, of course, because the trustees look after it all. The chief and the shaman and some lawyers and people like that. Elspeth said never ever to forget that I'm a figurehead, not a caretaker. It's the tribe that owns the land, not me.'

'And will you be going to San Lorenzo to meet the Kainu?'

Oliver flushed at the public mention of this secret ambition. With all the cold indifference he could muster he said cagily, 'I don't know. I might.'

'Thank you so much for talking to us, Oliver. And now in the studio we have Liberal Democrat MP Torquil Guthrie to discuss some of the implications of this extraordinary affair.'

Ollie's face wore much the same expression now as he made his way into the abbey, his brave attempt at nonchalance betrayed by the self-conscious pinkness of his ears. Morgan tried to meet his eye but he stared sternly past her and slid into his designated pew. All the performers had been given seats on the central aisle to facilitate the smooth running of the ceremony. Morgan found her place and sat down, suddenly very aware of the plain oak coffin with its heaped tribute of flowers. Inside that box it would be dark. She was unable to force her mind to penetrate that imagined darkness and touch the dead woman.

Instead she found herself repeating under her breath the lines she was soon to recite, like someone muttering a prayer. The *sotto voce* murmur of prayer was in fact going on all round her as the scattering of believers among the congregation bowed their heads, in that curiously respectable and shame-faced Anglican way. The rest were glancing around, spotting friends and identifying celebrities. All the same, there was an underlying sense of unease which marred the usual funeral atmosphere of sociability heightened by grief. People seemed nervously expectant, on edge. If Elspeth had been murdered in South America, Morgan thought savagely, they wouldn't be half so keyed up about it. It was a relief when the organ started. Morgan didn't know the piece. Something eminently suitable, not chosen, just laid on. The swell of sound was accompanied by stirrings and rustlings, magnified by the great stone echo chamber of the nave, as the assembled company gradually settled itself into attentive stillness. The west door creaked open and banged shut first once and then twice as a few latecomers hurried in.

Inspector Burdock was well aware that Fowler would regard his presence at the funeral as an insubordinate gesture. The Chief Superintendent was still smarting over the exoneration of Enoch Potter. He had been obliged to respond to the publicity stirred up by Torquil Guthrie with an unimpressive statement to the effect that the police had every

255

reason to believe that Dr Blair-Guthrie had been killed by an opportunistic burglar and were still following up all available leads in their efforts to find the culprit. If leads were indeed being followed, it was no longer Burdock who was following them. After Potter's release he had asked to be taken off the case. However, his memory of the victim and his anger at the thwarting of his attempts to find her killers were still too strong for him to think of missing the service, though he judged it would be wiser not to appear among the televised crowd of mourners. He had timed his entrance deftly and had just located a vacant seat when the heavy door was pushed open again and James and Libby Gilbert came in, walking stiffly and a little way apart as if anxious not to touch each other. Burdock hastily sat down and bent his head in simulated prayer. He had no good news to offer the Gilberts, despite being free now to devote all his energies to the hunt for little Ben.

He was aware that James Gilbert had had some kind of breakdown following the revelation that the police had been holding the wrong man and that he had been given extended leave by his hospital. Burdock privately doubted if he would ever work again. Cases of child-killing by strangers were rare, but Burdock had encountered enough of them in the course of his career to have a fair idea of what was going on inside James Gilbert's head. An obsessive need to know his son's whereabouts, even if those whereabouts were a grave, and an even stronger need for vengeance. Not justice, vengeance. Someone else must suffer for his pain. If possible, the perpetrator; but if not, then any available scapegoat who could be labelled with the crime. Enoch Potter had been accused of killing Ben, by the gutter press if not by the law, and to be accused of such a deed, however mistakenly, was to be, not guilty exactly, but something almost worse. Dirtied, so to speak, thought Burdock, unaware that the dead woman could have supplied him with the concept he was groping for. It must have been unbearable to see Potter reunited with his own child, all the more so because of Gilbert's rigid determination to remain civilised and rational under all circumstances. Well, it didn't look as if he was going to get justice, or vengeance either, and it was becoming increasingly likely that Ben would never be found. Burdock was unable even to begin to imagine what Libby must be feeling. Her expressionless face was a locked door behind which speculation could not venture.

By this time the organ music had come to an end in a plangency of solemn chords and the Vicar's opening words had ushered forward Torquil Guthrie. The entire congregation seemed to take a deep breath and shift a little in their seats. This was the moment they had all been waiting for, Burdock included. The audience could doubtless be divided into cock-up theorists who believed Fowler's version of events or something fairly like it and conspiracy theorists who bought

257

Guthrie's ingenious scenario. Burdock wasn't sure to what extent he bought it himself. He was certain, now, if only from Fowler's determination to warn him off, that Dr Blair-Guthrie had been under surveillance and that it had been incompetent spooks who had killed her when she discovered them ransacking her flat, but the idea that international mining interests plus the US government, eager to prop up General Paragual's dodgy regime, had together persuaded British Intelligence to target one awkward little old lady, and in Oxbourne of all places, was almost more than he could get his head round. Like nearly everyone else in the place, including the media contingent, he was expecting Guthrie to use the occasion to make some kind of public statement. Instead he described the hills round Blair Easton where his aunt had grown up and recited some lines full of moorland air and martyrs' graves and the calling of oddly named birds. He followed this up with a snatch from a Gaelic lament, almost chanting the mournfully incomprehensible phrases. He didn't offer to translate them and sat down, leaving the congregation restless and cheated of drama.

He was followed by Lady Buckhaven who spoke about Dr Blair-Guthrie's early career. She too avoided any mention of the murder, though, given her pugnacious involvement with third world causes, her very presence could be seen as making a point. It was Professor Kyle who put words to what everyone was thinking. Having read an extract from *Ritual and Reality*, Dr Blair-Guthrie's book about the Kainu, and spoken of her qualities as a teacher and scholar, he added quietly, 'We may not know for certain how she died, but we know of the risks that if need be she was prepared to run. She had the kind of stubborn and abiding courage on which, in the last analysis, all our liberties depend.'

Dr Byrd, aggressively stylish in black leather, spoke of the dead woman's clear sightedness and impatience with sentimentality and self-deception, before reciting a poem which some titled character had translated on his deathbed, and which struck Burdock as hardly suitable for performance in church.

'Let slavish souls lay by their fear,

Nor be concerned which way nor where

After this life they shall be hurled.

Dead, we become the lumber of the world,

And to that mass of matter shall be swept

Where things destroyed with things unborn are kept.'

The defiant lines, faultlessly pitched, reached effortlessly to the back of the building and fell on Burdock's ears like a spadeful of earth falling on a coffin lid. They reminded him somehow of a poem he had learnt at school. How did it go now? 'Rolled round in earth's diurnal course with rocks and stones and trees.' Gave you a real shiver, that did, though it was hard to say why. Something to do with that word diurnal perhaps. God knows what it meant. She would, of course, Dr Byrd. Could have been an actress, that one, if only she made herself look a bit less macho. Attractive woman, mind, he had to give her that.

As if disturbed by the leaden finality of the words, a baby broke into a thin wail and was vigorously joggled into silence before it could set off a whole chorus of infant howls. Burdock glanced across at Libby Gilbert and saw her face stiffen into a stone mask at the sound. Melanie Wilson, he thought. She's the only lead we've got left. She can't still be in a catatonic trance, can she? Pretty suspicious, at any rate, if she is. I'll get Sergeant Blossom to have another go in the morning, not that it will do any good. He's dead anyway, poor little beggar. Must be.

Dr Byrd came to the end of her piece and Oliver Cresswell started down the aisle carrying his violin. Bloody little show-off, thought Burdock. I suppose he was bound to put in his pennyworth. It'll be the Bach chaconne, I bet. The child seemed absurdly small beneath the towering pillars, despite his air of composure. His hair had been cut too short and the back of his neck looked thin and vulnerable. He's only a kid, thought Burdock, when all's said and done. And he was fond of the old girl, of course. Her and that flaming tomcat. Dr Byrd was walking back to her place now, her high-heeled boots stirring the echoes as she paced across the flagstones. She paused when she reached Oliver, as if at a prearranged signal. He gave her the violin and the bow and went on to the front empty handed.

Morgan knew what was about to happen. She had spent hours searching through Elspeth's tape collection and more hours coaching Ollie in voice production. As he handed over the violin, their eyes had met in a rare moment of mutual respect. In this small enterprise, at least, they were partners. Good on you, kiddo, she thought, sitting down beside Lin. Sock it to them.

Oliver turned in front of the coffin and faced the cameras and the mikes and the endless-seeming rows of people. He had planned exactly what he was going to say. His voice came out a bit croaky at first but then it settled as the importance of what he was about to do took hold of him.

'Elspeth belonged to the Kainu tribe and now I do too. They made her a hunter of the jaguar clan because she helped to fight some men who came to kill them. It was their way of saying she was as brave as a jaguar. In the tribe, when a hunter dies they sing to the ancestor spirits to take him into the spirit world, so I'm going to do that now for Elspeth.'

He paused and took a deep breath the way Morgan had taught him, feeling his tummy muscles supporting the column of air inside him, and tried to pitch the first notes in his head.

He had listened to the tape through his headphones dozens of times but these were words that could only be sung aloud once. Morgan had made him stand outside the kitchen door and sing Men of Harlech over and over while she leaned against the apple tree at the bottom of the garden. She had told him to imagine he was doing that when he sang in the abbey. Now that the moment was upon him, though, he knew that this had nothing to do with any living audience. He half closed his eyes to blank out the faces: Lin lost in her own thoughts, Morgan watching him with fierce complicity, Professor Kyle suddenly alert with scholarly interest, the Vicar mildly appalled at the intrusion of first atheism and now ancestor worship into his sanctuary, his mother slowly turning magenta under her veil. The stone pillars became trees soaring up to mesh their branches in the leafy canopy high overhead. His song was a spear which, if he hurled it skilfully enough, could pierce through the barrier between the worlds of flesh and spirit. He was a hunter, proud and naked in the forests of the night, the manhood beads shining around his neck. He took another breath without even thinking about it and opened his mouth and sang. The words rang out, thin and clear and alien, waking medieval echoes in the fretted stone, and no living ear understood them.

Morgan was thinking that she had just done her best to kill off the idea of an afterlife and here was Ollie resurrecting it, with her own active connivance. Professor Kyle was thinking that it provided a nice illustration of Elspeth's theories about the interface between ritual and reality. The Vicar was thinking it was a stunt in poor taste. Not a bad treble, though. Might be worth offering him a voice test. Burdock was thinking, that can't be what his mum had in mind. It's a wonder he didn't turn up in war paint and feathers. Lin was thinking about something else entirely. As the chant came to an end and Ollie blinked and focused once more on the packed pews in front of him, he saw her urgent face beckoning to him among the crowd. He walked back up the aisle to where Morgan was sitting, his violin balanced precariously on her knee. She gave him the quick, unsmiling glance that says mission accomplished and budged along to make room for him. He wedged himself uncomfortably into the narrow space next to the carved pew-end and leaned forward to get a clear view of Lin, who at once engaged him in animated conversation.

By now the service was drawing to an end. The Vicar was smoothing an oil-slick of emollient phrases over stormy waters. Lin and Ollie, silent but conspicuous, were blind to everything but their own engrossing discussion. Morgan, caught in the middle and trying to look as if she was concentrating on the Vicar's platitudes, could make out only the occasional sign. They seemed, mysteriously, to be talking about arithmetic and the colours of the rainbow. She contemplated digging her elbows into both sets of ribs in a shushing gesture but decided against it. You could take respect for convention too far, especially when convention took the form of an unctuous cleric publicly evading the fact that an elderly woman had been brutally murdered and her probable killers protected from justice by the establishment that had paid them to spy on her.

Instead, it was Lin who eventually prodded Morgan into attention and delivered a rapid and surprising set of instructions. Morgan mimed reluctance and bafflement but to no avail. Lin simply signed back, 'Don't argue about it, Bird. Just do it.'

'Jewish mother, yet,' Morgan muttered under her breath, recognising marching orders when she met them. Lin, lip-reading as she was meant to, gave her an old-fashioned look.

And then the Vicar's address had dribbled to a close, and the organ rang out with the opening chorale notes of Crimond. The coffin-bearers were hefting the long box onto their shoulders and everyone was rising to their feet, Scottish cousins and foreign connections, mainstream journalists and left-wing politicians, students and colleagues present and past, as the mortal remains of Elspeth Blair-Guthrie were carried up the central aisle and out through the west door. Morgan felt her throat contract and her eyes begin to prick and fought the feeling down. She had a task to perform, concentrate on that. As the coffin passed out of sight and the tension that had held the congregation together audibly slackened, she eased herself out of her seat and located her quarry. Over there, making for the south transept. Hastily she thrust the violin into Ollie's hands.

'Here's your fiddle, young Sherlock. See you.' Quickly but unobtrusively she began to edge through the crowd. Oliver, with Lin behind him, shoved a more blatant pathway for himself until he reached his mother. Daphne Cresswell drew a deep breath pregnant with maternal outrage at the sight of him but he didn't linger for recriminations.

'Here's my fiddle, Mum. I'm going home with Lin.'

Her shrill but fruitless cries of 'Ollie! *Ollie*! Come right back here to Mummy this instant!' were still echoing behind him as he elbowed his way out of the abbey.

CHAPTER THIRTY

Inspector Burdock strolled back to the station with a bad taste in his mouth. The funeral service had brought him starkly up against failure, his own personal failure to recover the missing child and the failure of the system he served to provide a murdered woman with justice. Torquil Guthrie might be able to go on drumming up a media circus for a few more weeks but even he must already know that the Blair-Guthrie affair was destined to become one of those long-running, mildly intriguing British mysteries which rate the occasional partisan book or independent television documentary. A dinner-table topic for the chattering classes. Only a handful of those closest to the case, like Dr Byrd and Guthrie himself, would continue to feel genuine anger about it. Burdock was aware that his own anger was partly due to the attack on his professional pride. He had told Lawrence Craik that it was his job to uphold the law and now he had been made a monkey of for attempting to do just that. Fowler, and the faceless mandarins who had used Fowler, had taken away his authority and left him feeling powerless and betrayed.

He was not best pleased to discover Oliver Cresswell pelting along behind him, full of some garbled tale about finding the vital clue.

'Not now, lad, if you don't mind. I'm not in the mood for games.'

Oliver, narrow chest heaving, refused to be brushed off. 'No, wait. Listen. Lin's just coming. She'll explain.'

Who the hell is Lin, thought Burdock tetchily. She proved to be a slight, intelligent-looking woman in her early forties, dressed like a Sunday school teacher and with long white-blonde hair carelessly pulled back in a bun.

She said abruptly, without preamble, 'We've found Ben Gilbert's pram.' Her voice had the uncontrolled, sing-song tones of the profoundly deaf.

'You have?' said Burdock, puzzled. 'I didn't know it was missing again.'

She peered intently at him as he spoke, then turned to Ollie, hands and face moving in vehement wordless speech.

'She says she can't lip-read properly because of your moustache.'

Taken aback, Burdock tugged self-consciously at a corner of the offending growth. 'Well, I'm not going to shave it off for her, lad,' he said stoutly. 'I'll tell you that for nothing.'

'Oh, don't worry,' said Oliver casually. 'I'll translate for you.'

Delighted to show off his party-trick, thought Burdock. As if he hadn't drawn enough attention to himself with that jungle book solo.

'All right,' he snapped, 'perhaps you could ask her what on earth she's on about. You've already had your picture all over the papers for finding that bloody pram.'

'Only it wasn't,' said Ollie cryptically. 'They'd been swapped.'

'What makes you think that? Or Miss... '

'Jensen.'

'Or Miss Jensen either.'

'It's because of the beads. It was Lin who worked it out.'

'All right, perhaps the pair of you had better come along to the station and tell me what this is all about.'

It took some time to disentangle the story, but eventually Burdock grasped that young Oliver had done a painting of the dead cat, complete with pram, and Miss Jensen had spotted that one detail in the painting didn't correspond to the pram on Octavia Castlemain's missing baby posters.

'You're asking me to believe you memorised the colours of the beads on that pram you found in Hangman's Wood?'

'Of course not. It was a sequence, like a sequence of numbers. I didn't have to learn it. I just remembered it, that's all.'

'And you can still remember it?'

'Of course I can. Pink blue yellow white red turquoise orange purple green. You can check.'

'But you didn't notice that the pram on the poster was different?'

'No, why should I? I never looked at it. I'm not interested in babies.'

'But now Miss Jensen thinks she's found the pram on the poster? Does she remember sequences too?'

'She remembers colours. She's a painter.'

'OK, so ask her the colours of the beads on the pram she found, would you, lad?'

Ollie translated with all the éclat of a boy conjurer about to pull a rabbit out of a hat. Miss Jensen said unhesitatingly, 'Red. Cyan. White. Orange. Violet. Rose. Blue. Green. Yellow.'

Burdock unpinned the photograph of Ben from his noticeboard and said, 'Well, that's not right for a start. This lot begins with yellow.'

Oliver relayed this. 'Other way round,' said Miss Jensen calmly. 'They unhook.'

'So what's to stop someone rearranging them?'

'The string is sealed at the ends. Babies swallow loose beads.'

Burdock scratched his head, trying to think it through. 'All right, let's take it that for some reason the kidnapper dumped the wrong pram. That doesn't prove that the one Miss Jensen thinks she's found has anything to do with Ben Gilbert. It's probably just a coincidence. I mean, there can't be all that many ways of arranging a few beads.'

Ollie said flatly, 'A hundred and eighty-one thousand, four hundred and forty.'

'How much? How do you work that out, sonny?'

'Factorial nine divided by two,' said Ollie, as if that should be self-evident even to Burdock.

'Come again? What's that when it's at home?'

Ollie sighed with exaggerated patience at this example of adult stupidity. 'Give me a pencil and a bit of paper and I'll show you.'

He scribbled down the sum and pushed the paper across the desk. Burdock pondered it, then let out his breath in a gust that stirred the fringes of his drooping moustache.

'OK, son, you've proved your point. So where did Miss Jensen see this blessed pram?'

Morgan, meanwhile, was reflecting that there is no such thing as silence. In the pauses of Rosalind's querulous monologue she found herself abnormally aware of the soft creaks and shiftings which always haunt a quiet house, the nervous rhythm of her own heartbeat, the distant singing of the blood in her ears. She told herself, sensibly, that she was listening out for the doorbell but in fact she knew, with a certainty as chill as the clammy sensation in the pit of her stomach, that she was listening for a breath, a whimper, another fainter heartbeat, or else for its hideous absence. She was listening for Ben Gilbert, hidden somewhere in that house. Ben Gilbert or all that remained of what had once been a human child. She realised that the horror that had taken possession of her went far beyond the fierce emotion she felt over Elspeth's death. At least she had the comfort of knowing that Elspeth had confronted her own possible fate as stoically as, at the last, she must have confronted her killers. This was something else, something that made Morgan's scalp crawl and her throat gag with bile.

Insistent in her mind's eye was a photograph she had once seen in a magazine, a neolithic baby excavated from the permafrost somewhere in Siberia, the leathery skin freeze-dried to the tiny skull, the empty eye-sockets staring blankly into eternity. It was an effort to keep responding to Rosalind's litany of complaint with appropriate murmurs of comprehension and sympathy. Rosalind must have a freezer

271

in her well-equipped kitchen. Was that where Ben now lay, pale and still in his shawl of ice? Did Rosalind herself have any idea what she had done? Christ, how much longer was it going to take before the police arrived? It was the waiting which was so intolerable. Up until now she had had to act, in both senses, and the need for resourcefulness and guile had numbed her imagination. Now there was nothing left to do except wonder when Burdock and his team would get here and what they would find when they did.

She had caught up with Rosalind just outside the abbey and collared her with the oiled smoothness of a taxi tout, firmly seizing the folded undercarriage of the pram and steering her towards the car. Rosalind had been startled and none too grateful but she had accepted the proffered lift home without protest. However it had been plain, before the end of the short journey, that Morgan was not going to find herself invited in. She had sat in the car watching Rosalind, burdened with Zeffie and the pram, retreating up the front path and into the house, then revved the engine noisily a few times and let it die. There was a tense couple of minutes in which she wondered whether Rosalind was going to respond to her urgent thumb on the doorbell. When her unwelcoming face finally appeared in the crack of the chained door, Morgan had delivered her lines with all the naturalness she could muster.

'I'm terribly sorry, Ros, but the car seems to have snuffed it and I've left my mobile at home. I didn't want it going off during the service. Do you mind if I come in and phone the AA?'

The phone-call had been trickier to fake. She had keyed in her own number, her back turned on Rosalind's conceivably suspicious gaze, and heard her own recorded voice saying, 'Morgan Byrd and Lin Jensen are unable to come to the phone right now...' Her awareness that her performance was being recorded didn't make her breezy account of engine failure any easier to pull off. Morgan tried to summon up a phantom receptionist, plummy-voiced and over-genteel but doing her best to be helpful.

'That's a pity,' she told this disembodied stereotype, her own voice sounding almost as brightly artificial. 'Oh well, not to worry. Thanks. Bye.' She handed the phone back to Rosalind with some relief. 'They've got a bit of a backlog, apparently, but she says they'll get here as soon as they can.'

That had been nearly an hour ago and since then Rosalind had talked, in a hesitant monotone punctuated by long sighing pauses, about her insomnia and her sinuses and the inconsiderateness of her absent husband; and all the while, as if her mother's catalogue of grievances had been a lullaby, Persephone Jane had slept peacefully under her string of gaudy plastic beads.

'No, but I do think it's selfish of him, Morgan. I really do. I mean, it may not matter to anyone else but I do have my own work too. And then there's the house to sort out and everything to see to. And when he knows I've never been properly well since Zeffie was born. I really do think it's inconsiderate. And he didn't even ask whether I wanted to live in that horrible place where anything could happen to Zeffie. All he cares about is himself. Himself and his work. I do think it's selfish of him. I really do.'

As she talked, she picked nervously at her fingernails and fiddled with the ends of her hair. The colourless voice seemed to loop round on itself in endless repetitions, making it hard to piece meanings together, but gradually it became clear what Rosalind was saying. She was leaving Oxbourne, leaving the country, soon and for good. Planning a final escape, presumably, from the terrible secret that she knew, or else refused to know, was hidden somewhere in that house or under the funereal laurels and junipers of the secluded garden.

When the doorbell rang, Morgan started like a dreamer roused from a nightmare and got hastily to her feet.

'I'll go. It'll be the AA.'

It was Burdock and Crewe and the woman officer who had questioned Ollie about finding Elspeth's corpse. Morgan stood aside in the doorway to let them through and nodded in the direction of the sitting-room. They filed past her in

274

purposeful silence. Morgan lingered in the hall, wondering whether she should go or stay. She could hear Inspector Burdock's measured tones, presumably repeating some official formula, and then a whimpering cry that must be Persephone Jane. She glanced down the garden path and saw, through the open gate, a police car parked outside with James and Libby Gilbert sitting in the back. She didn't see either what she could possibly say to them or how she could go by without a word. She turned and went back down the hall.

Rosalind was standing, as if in a tableau of the massacre of the innocents, with her wailing daughter clasped histrionically to her breast. Her face was a study of indignation and denial.

Burdock was saying sternly, 'Look, are you telling me those prams were swopped accidentally before your nephew disappeared? Because your sister-in-law claims that photo was taken only a few days before he vanished and you haven't been near her since.' Rosalind was transformed on the instant from a mother confronting Herod's brutal soldiers to a vixen cornered by the hounds, her lips curling back from her teeth in a panting snarl. The woman officer, meanwhile, was glancing around the room with a practised eye.

Suddenly she said, 'Hang on a minute, sir. I think we may be on to something.' She went over to a small white box half-concealed in a corner and pressed a button. At once the room was filled with a sound that Morgan had never imagined she would be glad to hear, the lusty, full-throated howling of a baby expressing its uninhibited fury with the world.

Rosalind's voice rose too in an agonised shriek. 'You can't take her away from me! Not again! Not this time! She's mine! She's mine!' Her arms tightened convulsively round Persephone Jane, who responded by adding her own howls to the cacophony from the baby alarm. Burdock and Crewe exchanged dubious glances, rattled by the unexpected pronoun. The woman officer went over and gently prised the child from Rosalind's grasp.

'Now, don't take on, dear. We just want you to show us where you've put the other kiddy. Come along now, there's a good girl. Your friend here will look after baby.' She deftly manoeuvred the crimson-faced infant into Morgan's unwilling arms and led Rosalind from the room.

Morgan sat down abruptly on the sofa, taken aback by the weight and intransigence of the enraged Zeffie, who at once began to arch her back spasmodically between yells in a determined effort to fling herself onto the floor. Almost awestruck, Morgan recast her idea of Rosalind, no longer an infanticidal monster but barely easier to comprehend than she had been before. This you can want two of? she thought incredulously as she grappled with the threshing, bawling creature on her knee. In the background, the baby alarm continued to howl. It seemed ungrateful, under the circumstances, to say, can't you switch off that bloody din. In the event it was Burdock who said it. Sergeant Crewe was turning over papers on an antique rosewood secretaire between the two tall windows and took no notice.

'Looks as if we got here just in time, sir. Seems she was planning to skip the country.' Then, as he continued to rummage, he gave a smothered exclamation. His face changed and he said anxiously to Morgan, 'Excuse me, miss, but could you tell me what that baby there is called?'

'Persephone, poor little bugger,' said Morgan shortly.

'Well, she wouldn't happen to have a twin sister, would she? Name of Flora Simonetta? Because if so, I think we may have just made a very embarrassing mistake.'

Burdock strode across the room and glanced at the pair of documents that Crewe held out to him but, before he could comment on this latest twist in the case, a voice came from the baby alarm.

'Are you there, sir? Could you send Crewe up to keep an eye on Mrs Gilbert for a minute? The kiddy looks fine but I'd like to get him into a clean nappy before we have the parents in to identify him.'

Burdock and Crewe exchanged involuntary glances. 'She said him, sir,' said Crewe hopefully. 'Sounds as if she's checked, too, if she knows the state of his nappy.'

He made for the door, then paused to look at Morgan and her furious charge. Suddenly cheerful and expansive, he said, 'If you don't mind me saying so, miss, it often helps if you jig them up and down a bit. Makes them think they're moving along, like. Back in prehistoric times, you see, babies would know to keep quiet when the tribe was on the move, but they'd kick up a fuss for food and that when they got to wherever they was going. Not that they had nappies in those days, of course,' he added reflectively as he left the room.

Gingerly, remembering how Rupert Allison had quieted Joshua during the funeral service, Morgan tried to follow his advice. Almost at once, Zeffie's yells began to slacken. She hiccupped into silence and expelled a dribble of white, cheesy vomit down the front of Morgan's black silk shirt.

The infant which was presently borne into the room by a relieved-looking Crewe appeared, to Morgan's unpractised eye, indistinguishable from the one she was holding. It had the same formless baby features and its scalp was similarly mottled under the downy hair with the flush of recently pacified rage. It was dressed in identical white frills and pink smocking.

Crewe said proudly, 'It's a boy,' and then heard himself and blushed. 'I mean, it's the missing kid all right, sir. She's been hiding him in the attic. Padded the place with blankets and mattresses to soundproof it.'

Burdock had been muttering into his phone to the driver of the police car. Now he raised a jocular eyebrow and said, 'Ever considered a career-change, Crewe? Go down a treat in the labour ward, you would.' Meanwhile, the woman officer was shepherding Rosalind Gilbert into the room, holding her firmly but not unkindly by the arm. Rosalind now had a grey and shadowy look which reminded Morgan uneasily of Melanie Wilson. She walked in a nervous shuffle, hanging her head. Burdock glanced at her and said, 'Sergeant, could you take Mrs Gilbert into the kitchen for a tick while we have the parents in, then take her out to the car.'

But before he had finished speaking there was a clatter of running feet and the door burst open. Libby Gilbert paused in the doorway for the length of one snatched breath, her gaze going hungrily round the room, then, with a display of maternal instinct which reminded Morgan of a nature documentary she had once seen about penguins, she made straight for her own chick which, strangely, broke into a desolate wail at the sight of her. Sergeant Crewe handed him over, beaming like a midwife, and for a moment all eyes, even Morgan's, were focused on the powerful icon of mother and child as Libby tenderly cradled and hushed her son.

It was only when Rosalind suddenly tore herself out of Sergeant Blossom's grasp that Morgan realised that James Gilbert, gaunt and formal in his dark suit, had entered the room. Without giving him a chance to approach his wife and child, Rosalind flung herself at him, pounding at his chest with her fists and screaming out violent accusations of desertion and heartless neglect. Libby was still oblivious to everything but Ben, but for a moment the other bystanders were united in imagining a lurid subplot of adultery and revenge. Then James said stiffly, 'I'm not responsible for how Andrew choses to behave, Ros. I'm his brother, not his double. He didn't ask my advice before he walked out.'

A sly and crazy smile slid over Rosalind's face. 'But it's all right now. Everything's going to be all right. He doesn't love that bitch any longer. I'm taking Flora and Zeffie out to join him and we'll all be together at last.'

James said sharply, 'Rosalind, stop this. Flora is dead.'

For a moment it was as if he had slapped her awake. Then Rosalind flashed back at him, 'If she's dead it's because you killed her.'

A pulse began to beat in James's temple but he held on to his professional self-control. 'Look, you have to be reasonable, Ros. She wasn't my patient. The unit did everything it could.'

'She's dead because you didn't save her. I asked you to. I begged you to. But you did nothing. Nothing.'

As formally as if at a case conference, James said, 'She was terribly brain-damaged. You know that, Ros. She couldn't have survived and she'd have had no kind of quality of life if she had.'

'You didn't give a shit about her quality of life and neither did Andrew. You didn't even try. And after she was dead the pair of you cut up those innocent monkeys just so you could experiment on somebody else's child.'

James had been holding her by the shoulders, trying to make her see reason by the force of physical contact, but now he let go of her as if she had spat in his face. He said slowly, 'It was you who sent that letter. How could you, Ros? How could you torture Libby like that when she was so worried about Benjie?'

The little scene, as tensely self-contained as if it was being acted on a stage, was unexpectedly broken by Libby's waspish voice.

'Oh shut up, James, for Christ's sake. Can't you see the state she's in?' Still clasping Ben she went over and put an arm round Rosalind and led her aside, murmuring soothingly, 'It's all right, Rosie. Don't worry. We'll sort it all out. You'll see.' Rosalind went with her like an automaton.

James said helplessly, 'I was concerned for you, that's all.'

'That's all?' said Libby, her voice rising shrilly. 'That's all? Too bloody right that's all! I was the one who worried about Benjie and you were the one who was too busy playing at doctors to notice that he'd gone. It's not as if you were ever at home when he was awake. I wonder you even recognise him. You'd have been closer to him if he was unconscious on the operating table. At least Andrew had the balls to run off with another woman. With you it's nothing but that bloody hospital. I reckon Rosie's got it just about right. You don't give a shit.'

She turned to Inspector Burdock, her manner suddenly level and conciliating, a middle-class woman employing the weapons of privilege on behalf of her own kind.

'I know this has all been a great deal of trouble for you, Inspector, but we really wouldn't want to press charges. Benjie's none the worse and you can see that my sister-in-law is ill. I'm sure that any psychiatrist would confirm that. She had pre-eclampsia, you see, so the twins had to be delivered too early. Flora only lived for ten days and they thought at one point that they were going to lose Zeffie too. It must have been eating away at her ever since until she didn't know what she was doing any more. I know you have to question her, but if you would just let me come with her so she doesn't have to feel she's all alone.'

Her confidential tone reduced the whole matter to a family affair and Burdock to a valued tradesman who could be trusted to smooth away any unpleasantness. On a different day, Burdock might have parried with a show of authority but the sick taste left by Dr Blair-Guthrie's funeral was still in his mouth and any triumph he might have felt at solving the kidnapping had been dissipated by the lack of recognition or gratitude, together with the shrewd suspicion that after the first rejoicing headlines the press would be clamouring for a public inquiry into why it had taken the police so long. He shrugged and said, 'As you wish. We'll need a medical check on young Ben here in any case. All right, Crewe, Cherry, let's get moving.'

As the little procession left the house, Libby called indifferently over her shoulder, 'Just keep an eye on Zeffie till I get back, would you, James.'

The silence after the door slammed shut was like the exhausted and wreckage-strewn calm that follows a gale. For one thankful moment, Morgan let herself believe that now she was free to hand over her unwelcome nursling and go. Then she caught sight of James Gilbert's immobile face. He was standing with fists clenched and shoulders rigid, seemingly as unaware of her presence as if he had been struck blind. With a wholly uncharacteristic leap of imaginative sympathy, she realised that he had not even been given the chance to touch his new-found son. To Morgan one baby was pretty much like another, but she knew that there was no way she could offer him the virtually identical Zeffie, as if in a barren travesty of consolation. She thought of her own grief for Elspeth, a whole person with a lifetime of wisdom and experience and memories now callously blotted out. How strange that it was possible to break your heart and let go of your sanity over the loss of a half-human little frog like the one she was holding on her lap. She looked down at the small fragile skull with an unwonted curiosity. Persephone, she thought. The girl who came back from the underground kingdom, leaving her other self, her twin sister, behind in the dark.

As if the idea of sorrow was contagious, Zeffie broke into a thin, bleak mewing, forlorn as the cry of an orphan lamb on a winter hillside. Mimicking an instinct that she had never expected to need, Morgan began to rock her to and fro and then to murmur words that had once served to comfort another, older child in the aftermath of his first real experience of cruelty and loss.

'Tyger, tyger, burning bright in the forests of the night, what immortal hand or eye could frame thy fearful symmetry.'

At the sound of this unlikely lullaby, James Gilbert slowly raised his hands to cover his face and began to weep in great retching, gulping sobs which burst their way violently out of him as if some inner demon was tearing him apart.

EPILOGUE

It was almost a year later that Channel 4 screened *Death of a Hunter*, their award-winning documentary about the Kainu, filmed by one of Elspeth's former students, now a successful telly anthropologist. The programme had been structured around Oliver Cresswell and the boy who had acted as proxy for him at his initiation and purported to show the coming together of two mutually alien worlds. To Morgan, sitting on the sofa beside Lin, both these worlds appeared equally fictitious. This kind of stylised glimpse of an exotically photogenic culture had always reminded her uneasily of David Attenborough displaying the charms of some creature on the verge of extinction. In any case, whatever the carefully staged encounter might have meant to Ollie and his solemn-faced tribal blood-brother, it could surely never be captured by such artfully deft camera-work and tactfully over-informative commentary. Perhaps for both boys, like children everywhere on whom adult convenience has willed a token and unrealisable friendship, it had merely been an experience of mutual shyness.

Ollie had said very little afterwards, even to Lin, about his meeting with the Kainu, but Morgan suspected that the reality of a stretch of rain forest of which his ownership was a legal fiction, and a tribe of which he was a member only in fantasy, must inevitably have been both a shock and a disappointment.

Or possibly that was just her own urban imagination recoiling from the ultimate version of closeness to nature. Sooner you than me, kiddo, she found herself thinking, as, under the gaze of the unseen film crew, Ollie was instructed in the mysteries of hunting for lizards with spear and blowpipe and regaled on monkey flesh and roasted yam. She could sense the spirit of Daphne Cresswell over the entire enterprise, distant but malign, preventing the involvement of her precious offspring in anything too dangerous or unhygienic. No chance of Ollie returning to Oxbourne with the facial tattoos that he probably yearned for. All the same, as the narrative unfolded, Morgan began to realise that she had underestimated the scope of the programme-maker's ambition. Little spikes of post-modern imagery began to intrude into the Edenic vistas of the forest. Glimpses of unreal cities – San Lorenzo, Chicago, London – and a montage of newspaper headlines in English and Spanish were backed by Ollie's voice, alarmingly pure and bloodless, singing the Kainu death chant at Elspeth's funeral.

In a hutted clearing, a grey-haired elder was telling a group of boys the origin myths of the tribe. Ollie sat among them, half naked, wearing a necklace of shell and feathers, his face absurdly beaky and pale among his brown-skinned companions, his expression as unwaveringly attentive as theirs. Cut into this scene were snatches of interviews from the phantasmagoric outer world which pressed insistently, with its greed and treachery, on the protected circle under the forest canopy. Andrew Gilbert in his lab at Gifford Pharmaceuticals. A former British intelligence agent, seen only from behind, silhouetted against a window. A San Lorenzan civil rights lawyer, his face reduced to a shifting mosaic of pixels, his voice deliberately drowned out by the interpreter's voice-over. A US mining magnate, regretful and rapacious as he contemplated the likely mineral wealth of the Kainu land. And finally, Torquil Guthrie in his office in the House of Commons, piecing together the chain of events which he believed had led to Elspeth's death. His anger had a weary quality to it by now, as had Morgan's. It was already clear that his campaign had made no difference; the culture of official secrecy was too ingrained. No charges would ever be brought in connection with Elspeth's death.

The camera had lost its innocence, searching the forest for signs of intrusion and corruption, finding here a battered transistor radio, there a half-empty packet of cheap cigarettes, lingering on the symptoms of poverty and disease. Ollie and his foster-brother, both wearing grubby shorts and T-shirts, sat side by side on a fallen tree-trunk and talked about their plans for the future. This was an Ollie that Morgan barely recognised, mature and serious and calmly confident of his ability to shape his own destiny. Not Ollie at all, in fact, but the boy the tribe knew as Oliverio, a boy entitled by his initiation to all the gravitas of manhood and at the same time too foreign for anyone to regard him as a freak.

'When I was younger I used to think I'd be an anthropologist like Elspeth, but now I think I'd rather be a doctor. They're going to need another doctor when Father Hernández retires.'

It was only when the invisible interviewer asked him if he was not then, after all, going to become Britain's youngest maths professor that a flash of the old Ollie emerged.

'No, I'm not, actually. Why should I? I'll have my PhD by the time I'm fifteen and I'll probably be bored with maths by then. Anyway, I want to learn Spanish. And history. Elspeth said you can't begin to understand a people until you understand the stories they tell about themselves.'

The other boy had grander dreams, fed by the siren voices of the radio. He jabbed his thumb towards his chest and said proudly, 'Futbolista! Copa Mundial!'

The moment of optimism was deliberately snuffed out, as the naivety of Ollie's adult-sounding ambition was put into bleak perspective by the man whose work he hoped to inherit. Father Hernández was every documentary-maker's idea of a

Catholic medical missionary, gaunt-faced and silver-haired, still clinging to the bare framework of his faith after a lifetime's unrewarding toil yet smiling with ironic sadness at the blows inflicted by an inscrutable providence on his unconverted flock.

'Now the Norteamericanos are saying that they want to buy the medicines of the tribe, yet the tribe is dying of fevers that I cannot buy the medicines to cure. Each year there is more contact with the outside world, enough to breed epidemics, not enough to build up immunities. At least I have been able to inoculate the children against whooping cough and measles, but nowadays there are sicknesses that I can do nothing to prevent, even with the help of God and his mother.

'There is the uncle of the boy Kerua, Oliverio's foster-brother. Ten years ago his wife was raped by a white man in the forest. She was then just fifteen years old. After that her children were born sickly and did not survive, and later she became ill. Last year she died and now her husband too is dying. Here in the forest, a man is considered old if he lives past fifty years, but now it is the young who die and the old who prepare their bodies for the fire.'

The camera had found the symbol it was searching for. As lovingly as a bluebottle on carrion, it settled on the dying man as he lay, sweating and emaciated, in his hammock. The women of his family were already painting and adorning his still-living corpse for its coming funeral with charcoal and red ochre and gaudy parrot feathers. Morgan watched, a disengaged and unwilling voyeur, as this death, ugly and actual as Elspeth's death, was crafted into a moving real-life art-object and distanced from her by the rectangle of the screen. Ollie, reduced to sullen childhood again, sat in the cabin of the motor launch, a pocket chess set in front of him, his disconsolate face propped on his bunched fists, as his foster-brother hauled branches from the forest and helped to build the pyre. The death chant rose again, this time from a dozen throats, as the hunters of the dead man's age set made smooth his passage into the spirit world.

As if the fatality had dissolved the traditional reticences of the genre, the next frame showed the scene being set for an interview with Aapuulo the tribal chief. Anthropologist, interpreter, cameras, mikes, carefully chosen background of smouldering embers and softly wailing women. The chief was a small man, heavily tattooed with interlacing spiral patterns which covered his face and arms. His chest was herringboned with ornamental scars. He stared into the camera with appropriately dark and unfathomable eyes. Morgan found the intonations of his voice impossible to decode, so that she was left trying to guess from the sub-titles, coloured as they inevitably were by the unexamined assumptions of the translator, whether his words expressed hope or despair about the likely future of the tribe. Noble savage-speak, yet, she thought, and found herself wondering uneasily if, at bottom, those had been Elspeth's assumptions too.

'My uncle's daughter's husband is dying from a fever brought by those who search for the yellow metal. His spirit is unhappy because it is too dangerous for us to drink his bones. The ancestors cannot help us in this because all these things are new to them. The old ways were good but now we must go down a different path. My sons must learn to count so that the gringos cannot cheat us. They must learn to speak Spanish. In this way the future will be different from the past.'

'So in a sense, then, Dr Blair-Guthrie's death was in vain?'

Aapuulo frowned and made a gesture to avert ill luck, or perhaps simply bad manners. 'She is with the ancestors. Among the Kainu we do not speak the names of those who have gone.'

'I'm sorry. I meant, if you are no longer able to preserve your traditional way of life ...'

A raised hand, courteously checking a folly before it could be uttered. 'Oliverio has told us of a beast with stripes, bigger than a jaguar, which lives wild in the forest until men come and catch it and put it in a cage. You are the same. You want to put us in a cage made out of our own customs. But we are the Kainu, the people. It may be that a time is coming when the tribe must die so that the people of the tribe can live.'

As the interview came to an end, the specially commissioned background music swelled slightly, signalling closure. The camera crew were seen packing up their kit, just as if filming was already finished. One last sequence, thought Morgan cynically, and it's a wrap.

On the riverbank, Ollie and Kerua touched foreheads and spoke a few ritual words of farewell. Among the Kainu, said the voice of the commentator, it is thought unlucky to linger over partings, lest the spirit of the one who goes becomes entangled with the spirits of those who remain. The group on the bank turned away at once and vanished among the trees but the boy kneeling in the stern went on looking steadily backwards as the launch slid away down the wide river and the credits rolled.